"Who do you think you are?" Penelope asked.

"Your husband," Connal said, "*Mrs*. Tremayne."

"Don't call me that. It's not my name."

"Oh, yes, it is. And you can forget that annulment. I won't sign the papers," he informed her.

"But, I don't want to be married to you!"

He lifted his eyebrows. "How do you know that? I haven't made love to you yet."

She went scarlet. Her fingers grasped the covers in a death grip, and she stiffened when he took a step closer to the bed, her eyes as wide as saucers in her flushed face.

He shook his head and made a clicking sound with his tongue. "My God, if you keep up this attitude, it's going to be impossible for us to have children together."

"I won't have children," Penelope whispered.

"Well, not like that," Connal murmured, grinning. "You *do* know how women get them?"

"Sure," she said. "From the hospital."

"That comes later," her reminded her. He smiled. "Afterward."

Dear Reader:

All of us here at Silhouette Books hope that you are having a wonderful summer, and enjoying all that the season has to offer. Whether you are vacationing, or spending the long, warm summer evenings at home, we wish you the best—and hope to bring you many happy hours of romance.

August finds our DIAMOND JUBILEE in full swing. This month features *Virgin Territory* by Suzanne Carey, a delightful story about a heroine who laments being what she considers "the last virgin in Chicago." Her handsome hero feels he's a man with a mission—to protect her virtue *and* his beloved bachelorhood at the same time. Then, in September, we have an extraspecial surprise—*two* DIAMOND JUBILEE titles by two of your favorite authors: Annette Broadrick with *Married?!* and Dixie Browning with *The Homing Instinct*.

The DIAMOND JUBILEE—Silhouette Romance's tenth anniversary celebration—is our way of saying thanks to you, our readers. To symbolize the timelessness of love, as well as the modern gift of the tenth anniversary, we're presenting readers with a DIAMOND JUBILEE Silhouette Romance each month, penned by one of your favorite Silhouette Romance authors.

And that's not all! This month don't miss Diana Palmer's fortieth story for Silhouette—*Connal*. He's a LONG, TALL TEXAN out to lasso your heart! In addition, back by popular demand, are Books 4, 5 and 6 of DIANA PALMER DUETS—some of Diana Palmer's earlier published work which has been unavailable for years.

During our tenth anniversary, the spirit of celebration is with us year-round. And that's all due to you, our readers. With the support you've given us, you can look forward to many more years of heartwarming, poignant love stories.

I hope you'll enjoy this book and all of the stories to come. Come home to romance—Silhouette Romance—for always!

Sincerely,

Tara Hughes Gavin
Senior Editor

DIANA PALMER

Connal

Silhouette *Romance*
Published by Silhouette Books New York
America's Publisher of Contemporary Romance

SILHOUETTE BOOKS
300 E. 42nd St., New York, N.Y. 10017

ISBN: 0-373-08741-1

First Silhouette Books printing August 1990

Printed in the U.S.A.

Books by Diana Palmer

DIANA PALMER

Connal is Diana Palmer's fortieth story for Silhouette Books! Also don't miss Diana's first published titles—available again in August 1990 in *Diana Palmer Duets* Books 4, 5 and 6—from Silhouette Books.

Underlined places are fictitious.

Chapter One

Because of the date, Penelope knew she wouldn't find him at the barn. That was where he usually was at this hour of the day. Any other time, C. C. Tremayne was always two steps ahead of his men in feeding the animals, especially with the drought that had turned the grass brown and brittle these past few weeks. The drought had been a bad break for her father. Even with the Rio Grande only a few miles away, water was a precious commodity and wells kept going dry, leaving the tanks they filled empty.

West Texas was usually hot in mid-September, but the wind was up and it was unseasonably cold this evening. Penelope had worn a jacket outside, and now she was glad she had. She shivered a little in the late afternoon chill.

It was just beginning to get dark, and Penelope knew that if she didn't get to C.C. before her father did, it was going to mean another nasty quarrel. Ben Mathews and his foreman had been at each other's throats enough in recent weeks and Penelope didn't want any more arguments. Her father always got bad-tempered when money was tight. Things couldn't be much worse right now.

C.C. was drinking. She knew it; it was that time of year again. Only Penelope knew the importance of that day in September in C.C.'s life. She'd once nursed him through a flu and a raging delirium and he'd told her everything. She didn't let on that she knew, of course. C.C.—he was called that, although nobody knew what the initials stood for—didn't like anyone knowing private things about him. Not even the girl who loved him more than life.

He didn't love Penelope. He never had, although she'd worshiped him since she was nineteen and he'd been hired as foreman when her father's oldest hand retired. It had only taken one long look at the lithe, lean, dark-eyed man with the hawkish features and unsmiling face for her to fall madly in love with him. It was three years later, and her emotions hadn't undergone any changes. Probably they never would. Penelope Mathews was pretty stubborn. Even her dad said so.

She grimaced when she saw the light on in the bunkhouse, and it was not even dark. The other men were out riding herd, because calving was in full swing and everybody was in a mean temper during calving. It meant long hours and little sleep, and it wasn't normal for any of the men to be in the bunkhouse at this hour of the day. That meant it had to be C.C., and he had to be drinking. And liquor was one thing Ben Mathews wasn't about to tolerate on his ranch, not even when it was being abused by a man he liked and respected.

She brushed back her light reddish-brown hair and nibbled on her full lower lip. She had her long, wavy hair in a ponytail and it was tied with a velvet ribbon that just matched her pale brown eyes. She wasn't a pretty girl, but she had a nice figure even if it was a little on the plump side. Not overweight, just rounded, so that she filled out her jeans nicely. Her hair was almost red-gold when the sun hit it, and she had a line of freckles over her straight nose. With a little work, she could have been lovely. But she was a tomboy. She could ride anything and shoot as well as her father. Sometimes she wished she looked like Edie, the wealthy divorcee C.C. dated frequently. Edie was a dish, all blond and blue-eyed and bristling with sophistication. She seemed an odd choice for a ranch foreman, but Penelope tried not to think about it. In her mind, she knew the reason C.C. dated Edie and it hurt.

She paused at the door of the bunkhouse and rubbed nervously at her jeans, tugging her nylon jacket closer against the cold wind. She knocked.

There was a hard thud. "Go away."

She knew the curt, uncompromising tone and sighed. It was going to be a long day.

Her gloved hand pushed open the door and she stepped into the warmth of the big common room where bunks lined the wall. At the far end was a kitchen arrangement where the men could have meals cooked. Nobody stayed here much. Most of the men were married and had homes on the ranch, except C.C. But during roundup and calving, the new men who were hired on temporarily stayed here. This year there were six, and they filled the building to capacity. But they'd be gone within a week, and C.C. would have the bunkhouse to himself again.

C.C. was leaning back in a chair, his mud-caked boots crossed on the table, his hat cocked over one dark eye, hiding most of his dust-streaked dark hair, his lean hands wrapped around a whiskey glass. He tilted the hat up, peered at Penelope with mocking derision and jerked it down again.

"What the hell do you want?" he asked in his curt drawl.

"To save your miserable skin, if I can," she returned in equally cutting tones. She slammed the door, skinned off her coat to reveal the fluffy white sweater underneath, and went straight to the kitchen to make a pot of coffee.

He watched her with disinterested eyes. "Saving me again, Pepi?" he laughed mockingly, using the nickname that everyone called her. "What for?"

"I'm dying of love for you," she muttered as she filled the coffeepot. It was the truth, but she made it sound like an outrageous lie.

He took it that way, too, laughing even louder. "Sure you are," he said. He threw down the rest of the contents of his glass and reached for the whiskey bottle.

Pepi was faster. She grabbed it away, something she'd never have managed if he'd been sober, and drained it into the sink before he could stagger to his feet.

"Damn you, girl!" he said harshly, staring at the empty bottle. "That was the last I had!"

"Good. I won't have to tear the place apart looking for the rest. Sit down and I'll make you some coffee. It will get you on your feet before Dad finds you," she mumbled. She plugged in the pot. "Oh, C.C.," she moaned, "he's combing the hills for you right now! You know what he'll do if he finds you like this!"

"But, he won't, will he, honey?" he chided, coming up all too close behind her to take her shoulders and draw her back against the warm strength of his lean body. "You'll protect me, like always."

"Someday I won't be in time," she sighed. "And then what will become of you?"

He tilted her worried eyes up to his, and little shudders ran through her body. He'd never touched her except in amusement or at a dance. Her heart had fed just on the sight of him, from a distance. He was very potent this close, and she had to drop her eyes to his lean cheeks to keep him from knowing that.

"Nobody ever gave a damn except you," he murmured. "I don't know that I like being mothered by a girl half my age."

"I'm not half your age. Where are the cups?" she asked quietly, trying to divert him.

He wasn't buying it. His lean fingers brushed back loose strands of her hair, making her nerves sit up and scream. "How old are you now?"

"You know very well I'm twenty-two," she said. She had to keep her voice steady. She looked up deliberately to show him that he wasn't affecting her, but the smoldering expression in those black eyes caught her off guard.

"Twenty-two to my thirty. And a damned young twenty-two," he said slowly. "Why do you bother with me?"

"You're an asset around here. Surely you know how close we were to bankruptcy when you got hired?" she asked on a laugh. "Dad owes a lot to your business sense. But he still hates liquor."

"Why?"

"My mother died in an automobile accident the year before you came here," she said. "My father had been drinking and he was behind the wheel at the time." She tugged against his disturbing hands and he let her go.

She looked through the cabinets and found a white mug that wasn't broken or chipped. She put it down by the coffeepot and filled it, and then she took it to C.C., who had sat down and was rubbing his head with his lean hands at the table.

"Head hurt?" she asked.

"Not nearly enough," he said enigmatically. He took the mug and sipped the thick black liquid. He glared at it. "What in hell did you put in here, an old boot?"

"Twice the usual measure, that's all," she assured him as she sat down beside him. "It will sober you up quicker."

"I don't want to be sober," he said shortly.

"I know that. But I don't want you to get fired," she returned, smiling pertly when he glared at her. "You're the only person on the place except Dad who doesn't treat me like a lost cause."

He studied her smooth features, her soft dark eyes. "Well, I guess that makes us two of a kind, then. Because you're the first person in years who gave a damn about me."

"Not the only one," she corrected, smiling in spite of her feelings as she added, "Edie cares, too."

He shrugged and smiled faintly. "I guess she does. We understand each other, Edie and I," he murmured quietly, his eyes with a faraway look. "She's one of a kind."

In bed, she probably was, Pepi thought, but she couldn't give herself away by saying so. She got up and brought the coffeepot to refill his cup.

"Drink up, pal," she said gently. "The vigilantes aren't far away."

"I feel more steady now," he said after he'd finished the second cup. "On the outside, anyway." He lit a cigarette and blew out a thick cloud of smoke, leaning back wearily in the chair. "God, I hate days like this."

She couldn't admit that she knew why without incriminating herself. But she remembered well enough what he'd said, and the way he'd screamed when the memory came back in a nightmare delirium. Poor man. Poor, tortured man. He'd lost his wife and his unborn child on a white-water rafting trip that he'd had the misfortune to survive. As near as she could tell, he'd blamed himself for that ever since. For living, when they hadn't.

"I guess we all have good ones and bad ones," she said noncommittally. "If you're okay, I'll get back to my cooking. Dad's reminded me that he's due an apple pie. I've been baking half the afternoon."

"You're a domestic little thing, aren't you?" he asked strangely, searching her eyes. "Is Brandon coming to see you tonight?"

She blushed without knowing why. "Brandon is the vet," she said shortly. "Not my boyfriend."

"You could use a boyfriend, tidbit," he said unexpectedly, his eyes narrowing, his frown deepening as he fingered the empty mug. "You're a woman now. You need more than companionship from a man."

"I know what I need, thanks," she replied, rising. "You'd better stick your head in a bucket or something and see if you can get that bloodshot look out of your eyes. And for heaven's sake, swallow some minty mouthwash."

He sighed. "Anything else, Mother Mathews?" he asked sarcastically.

"Yes. Stop getting drunk. It only makes things worse."

He stared at her curiously. "You're so wise, aren't you, Pepi?" he asked cuttingly. "You haven't lived long enough to know why people drink."

"I've lived long enough to know that nobody ever solved a problem by running away from it," she returned, glaring back when his eyes started flashing black fire at her. "And don't start growling, either, because it's the truth and you know it. You've spent years living in the past, letting it haunt you. Oh, I don't pretend to know why," she said quickly when he began to eye her suspiciously, "but I know a haunted man when I see one. You might try living in the present, C.C. It's not so bad. Even at calving time. And just think, you have roundup to look forward to," she added with a wicked grin. "See you."

She started out the door without her jacket, so nervous that she'd given herself away that she hardly missed it until the wind hit her.

"Here, you'll freeze," he said suddenly, and came toward her with the jacket in his hand. "Put this on."

Unexpectedly he held it for her and didn't let go even when she was encased in it. He held her back against his chest, both lean hands burning through the sleeves of the coat, his chin on the top of her head.

"Don't bruise your heart on me, Pepi," he said quietly, with such tenderness in his deep voice that her eyes closed instinctively at the tone. "I don't have anything left to give you."

"You're my friend, C.C.," she said through her teeth. "I hope I'm yours. That's all."

His hands contracted for a minute. His chest rose and fell heavily. "Good," he said then, and let her go. "Good. I'm glad that's all there is to it. I wouldn't want to hurt you."

She opened the door and glanced back, forcing a smile to her lips even though he'd just destroyed all her dreams. "Try some of Charlie's chili peppers next time you feel like a binge," she advised. "The top of your head will come off just as fast, but you won't have a hangover from it."

"Get out of here!" he grumbled, glaring at her.

"If I see Dad, I'll tell him you're getting a snack, before you feed the livestock," she returned, grinning. She closed the door quickly and she heard him curse.

Her father was already home when she got there. He glared at her from the living room, her mirror image except for his masculinity and white hair.

"Where have you been?" he demanded.

"Out counting sheep," she said innocently.

"Sheep or one black one named C.C.?"

She pursed her lips. "Well..."

He shook his head. "Pepi, if I ever catch him with a bottle, he's through here, no matter how good a foreman he is," he said firmly. "He knows the rules."

"He was making himself a snack in the bunkhouse," she said. "I just poked my head in to ask if he'd like some of my...excuse me, *your*...apple pie."

He scowled fiercely. "It's my pie. I'm not sharing it!"

"I made two," she said quickly. "You old reprobate, you'd never fire C.C. You'd shoot yourself first and we both know it, but save your pride and say you'd fire him if it makes you feel better," she told him as she stripped off her jacket.

He finished lighting his pipe and glanced at her. "You'll wear your heart out on him, you know," he said after a minute.

Her back stiffened. "Yes. I know."

"He's not what he seems," he continued.

She turned, eyeing him warily. "What do you mean?"

"You tell me." He stared at the window, where snow was touching the pane under the outside lights. "He drove in here without a past at all. No references. No papers. I gave him a job on the strength of my instinct and his very evident ability with animals and figures. But he's no more a line-riding cowboy than I am a banker. He's elegant, C.C. is. And he knows business in an uncommon way for a poor man. You mark my words, girl, there's more to him than what shows.''

"He does seem out of place at times,'' she had to admit. She couldn't tell him the rest—that she knew why C.C. was out here on a ranch in the middle of nowhere. But even she hadn't learned from her involuntary eavesdropping during his delirium why he'd left that shadowy past. He'd come from money and he'd suffered a tragic loss, she knew that, and he was afraid to risk his heart again. That didn't stop Pepi from risking hers, though. It was far too late for any warning.

"He could be anything, you know,'' he said quietly, "even an escaped convict.''

"I doubt that.'' She grinned. "He's too honest. Remember when you lost that hundred-dollar bill out in the barn, and C.C. brought it to you? I've seen him go out of his way to help other cowboys who were down on their luck. He's got a temper, but he isn't cruel with it. He growls and curses and the men get a little amused, but it's only when he's fighting mad that they run for the hills. And even then, he's in complete control. He never seems to lose it.''

"I've noticed that. But a man in that kind of control, all the time, may have a reason,'' he reminded her. "There are other men. Don't take chances.''

"You old faker,'' she muttered. "You're always pushing me at him.''

He threw up his hands. "I like him. But I can afford to. You understand what I mean?''

She grimaced. "I guess so. Okay. I'll let Brandon take me to the movies, how about that?"

He made a face. "What a consolation prize," he grumbled. "The poor man's a clown. How he ever got through veterinary school is beyond me, with his sense of humor! He's the kind of man who would show a stuffed cow at a championship cattle show."

"My kind of man, all right," she said fervently, smiling. "He's uncomplicated."

"He's a wild man," he countered.

"I'll tame him," she promised. "Now let me get those apple pies finished, okay?"

"Okay. But I'll take C.C.'s to him," he added gently. "I want to see for myself if he's eating."

She stuck her tongue out at him and went to the kitchen, sighing her relief once she was out of sight.

Chapter Two

Brandon Hale was a carrot-topped maniac, and in his spare time, he was a veterinarian. Pepi adored him. Probably if her heart hadn't been appropriated by C.C., she might have married Brandon one day.

He came by just as Pepi and her father were sitting down to the supper table.

"Oh, boy, apple pie." Brandon grinned, staring at the luscious treat Pepi had made. "Hello, Mr. Mathews, how are you?"

"Hungry," Ben said shortly. "And don't eye my apple pie. I'm not sharing it."

"But you will, won't you?" Brandon leaned down. "I mean, considering that you need your new calves inspected and that sick bull treated, and those inoculations given, with roundup on the way..."

"Damn, boy, that's hitting below the belt," Ben groaned.

"Just one little slice," Brandon said. "the size of a knife blade..."

"Oh, all right, sit down." The older man sighed. "But I hope you know I wouldn't share it with just anybody. And if you don't stop coming over here at night without a reason, you'll have to marry Pepi."

"I'd be delighted," Brandon said, winking at Pepi from his pale blue eyes. "Name the day, honey."

"The sixth of July, twenty years from now," she promised, passing the corn. "I expect to live a little before I settle down."

"You've already lived twenty-two years," her father remarked. "I want grandchildren."

"You have them yourself," Pepi invited. "I've been thinking about joining the Peace Corps."

Ben almost dropped his coffee cup. "You've what?"

"It would be something to broaden my horizons," she said. Not to mention getting her away from C.C. before she slipped up and bared her aching heart to him. Today had been a close call. He seemed to be suspicious of all the attention she gave him, and worried that he couldn't return her affections. It was getting too much for her. A year away might ease the pain.

"You could get killed in one of those foreign places," her father said shortly. "I won't let you."

"I'm twenty-two," she reminded him with a grin. "You can't stop me."

He sighed angrily. "Who'll cook and keep house and—"

"You can hire somebody."

"Sure." Her father laughed.

That brought home the true situation, and she felt instantly regretful that she'd brought it up. "I won't go right away," she promised. "And don't worry, things will get better."

"Pray for rain," Brandon suggested between bites. "Everybody else is. I've never seen so many ranchers in church."

"I've seen prayers work miracles," Ben remarked, and launched into some tales that kept Pepi's mind off C.C.

After they'd finished off half of Pepi's apple pie, Brandon went out with her father to check the sick bull. "I don't usually do night work when I can get out of it," Brandon told Pepi. "But for an apple pie like that, I'd come out to deliver a calf at three in the morning."

"I'll remember that," she said pertly, grinning.

"You're cute," he said. "I mean that. You're really cute, and if you ever want to propose matrimony, just go ahead. I won't even play hard to get."

"Thanks. I'll keep you in mind, along with my other dozen suitors," she said lightly.

"How about a movie Friday night? We'll run over to El Paso and eat supper before we go to the theater."

"Terrific," she agreed. He was loads of fun and she needed to get away.

"I won't get back until midnight, I guess," her father called out. "After we check that bull down at the Berry place, I want to look over Berry's books before the tax man gets them. Don't wait up."

"Okay. Have fun," she called back. It was a joke between them, because Jack Berry kept books that would have confounded a lawyer. It was almost estimated tax time, and Jack was the ranch's only bookkeeper. They should have hired somebody more qualified, but Jack was elderly and couldn't do outside work. Her father had a soft heart. Rather than see the old man on welfare, Ben had hired him to keep the books. Which meant, unfortunately, that Ben had to do most of the figuring over again at tax time. His soft heart was one reason the ranch was in the hole. He didn't really have a business head like his own father had possessed. Without C.C.'s subtle guidance, the ranch would have gone on the auction block three years ago. It still might.

C.C. She frowned, turning toward the back door. She was worried about him. He hadn't seemed too drunk when she'd gone to check on him earlier, and that was unusual. His yearly binges were formidable. She'd better give him another look, before her father thought to check him out at midnight.

The bunkhouse was filling up. There were three men in it, now, the newest temporary hands. But C.C. wasn't there.

"He was pretty tight-lipped about where he was going, Miss Mathews," one of the men volunteered. "But I'd guess he was headed into Juárez from the direction he took."

"Oh, boy," she sighed. "Did he take the pickup or his own car?"

"His own car—that old Ford."

"Thanks."

It was a good thing she drove, she thought angrily. One of these days she'd be gone, and who'd take care of that wild-eyed cowboy then? The thought depressed her. He wouldn't have any trouble finding somebody to do that, not with his looks. And there was always Edie.

She turned off on the road that led to the border. The official at the border remembered the big white Ford—there hadn't been a lot of traffic across, since it was a weekday night. She thanked him, went across and drove around until she found the white Ford parked with characteristic haphazardness in a parking space. She pulled in beside it and got out.

Fortunately she hadn't taken time to change. She was wearing jeans and a checked shirt with a pullover sweater and boots, just the outfit for walking around at night. She was a little nervous because she didn't like going places alone after dark. Especially the kind of place she was sure C.C. was going to be in. Too, she was worried in case her father came home and needed to ask her anything. Her closed bedroom door might fool him into thinking she was just asleep, but if he saw the pickup missing, he might get suspicious. She didn't want him to fire C.C. He liked the man, but if C.C. didn't tell him why he was drinking—and C.C. wouldn't—then her father was very likely to let him go anyway.

There was a bar not a block away from where she parked. She had a feeling that C.C. was in it, but when she looked inside, there were mostly Mexican men and only one or two young Americans. She walked the streets, peeking into bars, and almost got picked up once. Finally, miserable and worried, she turned and started back to the truck. On the way, she glanced into that first bar again—and there he was, leaning back in a chair at a corner table.

She walked in and went back to the corner table.

"Oh…'' C.C. let out a word that he normally wouldn't have. He was cold and dangerous looking now, not the easily handled man of a few hours ago. She knew that her old tactics wouldn't work this time.

"Hi,'' she said gently.

"If you're here to drag me back, forget it,'' he drawled, glaring at her from bloodshot eyes. There was a half-empty tequila bottle on the table and an empty glass beside it. "I won't go.''

"It's hot in here," she remarked, feeling her way. "Some air might help you."

He laughed drunkenly. "Think so? Suppose I pass out, tomboy. Will you throw me over your shoulder and carry me home?"

That hurt. He made her out to be some female Amazon. Perhaps that was how he thought of her—as just one of the boys. But she smiled. "I might try," she agreed.

He studied her with disinterested brevity. "Still in jeans. Always wearing something manly. Do you have legs, tomboy? Do you even have breasts—?"

"I'll bet you can't walk to the car by yourself," she cut him off, trying not to blush, because his voice carried and one or two of the patrons were openly staring their way.

He stopped what he was saying to scowl at her. "The hell I can't," he replied belligerently.

"Prove it," she challenged. "Let's see you get there without falling flat on your face."

He muttered something rough and got to his feet, swaying a little. He took out a twenty-dollar bill and tossed it onto the bar, his hat cocked arrogantly over one eye, his tall, lithe body slightly stooped. "Keep the change," he told the man.

Pepi congratulated herself silently on her strategy as he weaved out onto the street. He took off his hat and wiped his forehead hesitantly.

"Hot," he murmured. He shook his head, his breath coming hard and heavy. He turned to look at Pepi, frowning slightly. "I thought we were going for a walk."

"Sure," she said.

"Come here, then, sweet girl," he coaxed, holding out his arm. "I can't let you get lost, can I?"

It was the liquor talking, and she knew it. But it was so sweet to have his arm around her shoulder, his head bent to hers, his breath against her forehead. Even the scent of the tequila wasn't that unpleasant.

"So sweet," he said heavily, walking her away from the car, not toward it. "I don't want to go home. Let's just walk the night away."

"C.C., it's dangerous in this part of the city," she began softly.

"My name . . . is Connal," he said abruptly.

That was faintly shocking, to know that he had a real name. She smiled. "It's nice. I like it."

"Yours is Penelope Marie," he laughed roughly. "Penelope Marie Mathews."

"Yes." She hadn't known that he knew her full name. It was flattering.

"Suppose we change it to Tremayne?" he asked, hesitating. "Sure, why not? You're always looking after me, Penelope Marie Mathews, so why don't you marry me and do the thing right?" While she was absorbing the shock, he looked around weavingly. "Aha, sure, there's one of those all-night chapels. Come on."

"C.C., we can't . . . !"

He blinked at her horrified expression. "Sure we can. Come on, honey, we don't have to have any papers or anything. And it's all legal."

She bit her lower lip. She couldn't let him do this, she thought, panicking. When he sobered up and found out, he'd kill her. Not only that, she wasn't sure if a Mexican marriage was binding; she didn't know what the law was.

"Listen, now," she began.

"If you won't marry me," he threatened with drunken cunning, "I'll shoot up a bar and get us landed in jail. Right now, Pepi. This minute. I mean it."

Obviously he did. She gave in. Surely nobody in his right mind would marry them with him in that visibly

drunken condition. So she went along with him, worried
to death about how she was going to get him home. But
she knew that he owned a Beretta and had a permit for it,
and she couldn't be sure that he didn't have it on him.
God forbid that he should shoot somebody!

He dragged her into the wedding chapel. Unfortunately the Mexican who married them spoke little En-
glish, and Pepi's halting Spanish was inadequate to
explain what was going on. C.C., she recalled, spoke the
language fluently. He broke in on her stumbling expla-
nation and rattled off something that made the little man
grin. The Mexican went away and came back with a Bi-
ble and two women. He launched into rapid-fire Spanish, cueing first Pepi and then C.C. to say *si* and then he
said something else, grinned, and then a terrified Pepi
was being hugged and kissed by the women. C.C.
scrawled his signature on a paper and rattled off some
more Spanish while the little man wrote a few other
things on the paper.

"That's all there is to it." C.C. grinned at Pepi. "Here.
All nice and legal. Give me a kiss, wife."

He held out the paper, took a deep breath, and slid to
the floor of the chapel.

The next few minutes were hectic. Pepi finally managed to convey to the Mexican family that she had to get
him to the car. They brought in a couple of really mean-
looking young men who lifted C.C. like a sack of feed
and carried him out to the parking lot. Pepi had him put
in the pickup truck. She handed the boys two dollar bills,
which was all she had, and tried to thank them. They
waved away the money, grinning, when they noticed the
beat-up, dented condition of the old ranch pickup.
Kindred spirits, she thought warmly. Poor people al-

ways helped each other. She thanked them again, stuck the paper in her pocket, and started the truck.

She made it to the ranch in good time. Her father's Jeep was still gone, thank God. She backed the pickup next to the bunkhouse, where it wasn't visible from the house, and knocked on the door.

Bud, the new hand she'd spoken to earlier, answered the knock. Apparently the men had been asleep.

"I need a favor," she whispered. "I've got C.C. in the truck. Will you toss him on his bunk for me, before my dad sees him?"

Bud's eyebrows rose. "You've got the boss in there? What's wrong with him?"

She swallowed. "Tequila."

"Whew," Bud whistled. "Never thought of him as a drinking man."

"He isn't, usually," she said, reluctant to go into anything more. "This was an unfortunate thing. Can you do it? He's heavy."

"Sure I can, Miss Mathews." He followed her out in his stocking feet, leaving the bunkhouse door open. "I'll try not to wake the other men. They're all dead tired, anyway. I doubt they'd hear it thunder."

"Heavens, I hope not," she said miserably. "If my dad sees him like this, his life's over."

"Your dad don't like alcohol, I guess," Bud remarked.

"You said it."

She opened the pickup door. C.C. was leaning against it, sound asleep and snoring. Bud caught him halfway to the ground and threw him over his shoulder in a fireman's lift. C.C. didn't even break stride; he kept right on snoring.

"Thanks a lot, Bud," Pepi grinned.

"My pleasure, Miss. Good night."

She climbed into the pickup, parked it at the back of the house, and rushed upstairs to bed. Her father would be none the wiser, thank God.

She undressed to get into her gown, and a piece of paper fell to the floor. She unfolded it, and found her name and that of Connal Cade Tremayne on it along with some Spanish words and an official-looking signature. It didn't take much guesswork to realize that it was a marriage license. She sat down, gazing at it. Well, it wasn't worth the paper it was written on, thank God. But she wasn't about to throw it away. In days to come, she could dream about what it could have meant if it had been the real thing. If C.C. had married her, wanted her, loved her. She sighed.

She put the license in her drawer and she laid down on the bed. Poor man, perhaps his ghosts would let him rest for a while now. She wondered how much of tonight he was going to remember, and hoped he wouldn't be too furious at her for going to get him or for leaving his dilapidated old Ford in Juárez. But with any luck, the old car would be fine, and he could get somebody to go with him to get it when he sobered up. Anyway, he ought to be grateful that she went after him, she assured herself. With winter coming on, it might be hard to get a new job. She didn't want to lose him. Even worshiping him from afar was better than never seeing him again. Or was it?

The next morning, she woke up with a start as a hard knock sounded on her door.

"What is it?" she asked on a yawn.

"You know damned good and well what it is!"

That was C.C. She sat up just as he threw open the door and walked in. Her gown was transparent and low-cut, and he got a quick but thorough look at her almost bare breasts before she could jerk the sheet up to her throat.

"C.C.!" she burst out. "What in heaven's name are you doing!"

"Where is it?" he demanded, his eyes coldly furious.

She blinked. "You'll have to excuse me, I don't read minds."

"Don't be cute," he returned. He was looking at her as if he hated her. "I remember everything. I'm not making that kind of mistake with you, Pepi Mathews. I may have to put up with being mothered by you, but I'll be damned if I'll stay married to you when I'm cold sober. The marriage license, where is it?"

It was a golden opportunity. To save his pride. To save her flimsy relationship with him. To spare herself the embarrassment of why she'd let him force her into the ceremony. Steady, girl, she told herself. The marriage wasn't legal in this country, she was reasonably sure of that, so there would be no harm done if she convinced him it had never happened.

"What marriage license?" she asked with a perfectly straight face and carefully surprised eyes.

Her response threw him. He hesitated, just for an instant. "I was in Mexico. In Juárez, in a bar. You came to get me... We got married."

Her eyes widened like saucers. "We did what?"

He was scowling by now. He fumbled a cigarette out of his pocket and lit it. "I was sure," he said slowly. "We went to this little chapel and the ceremony was all in Spanish... There was a paper of some kind."

"The only paper was the twenty-dollar bill you gave the bartender," she mused. "And if it hadn't been for Bud whats-his-name helping me get you to bed last night, you wouldn't still be working here. You know how Dad feels about booze. You were really tying one on."

He stared at the cigarette, then at her, intently. "I couldn't have imagined all that," he said finally.

"You imagined a lot of things last night," she laughed, making a joke out of it. "For one, that you were a Texas ranger on the trail of some desperado. Then you were a snake hunter, and you wanted to go out into the desert and hunt rattlers. Oh, I got you home in the nick of time," she added, lying through her teeth with a very convincing grin.

He relaxed a little. "I'm sorry," he said. "I must have been a handful."

"You were. But, no harm done," she told him. "Yet," she added, indicating the sheet under her chin. "If my father finds you up here, things could get sticky pretty fast."

"Don't be absurd," he replied, frowning as if the insinuation disturbed him. "You're only a little tomboy, not a vamp."

Just what he'd said last night, in fact, along with a few other references that had set off her temper. But she couldn't let on.

"All the same, if you and Dad want breakfast, you'd better leave. And your car is still in Juárez, by the way."

"Amazing that it made it that far," he murmured dryly. "Okay. I'm sorry I gave you a hard time. Do I still get breakfast?"

She relaxed, too, grateful that she didn't have to lie anymore. "Yes."

He spared her one last scowling glance. "Pepi, you've got to stop mothering me."

"This was the last time," she promised, and meant it.

His broad shoulders rose and fell halfheartedly.
"Sure." He paused at the open door with his back to her.
"Thanks," he said gruffly.

"You'd have done it for me," she said simply.

He started to turn, thought better of it, and went out,
closing the door behind him.

Pepi collapsed on the pillow with a heartfelt sigh. She'd
gotten away with it! Now all she had to do was find out
just how much trouble she was in legally with that sham
marriage.

Chapter Three

It took Pepi half the next day to work up enough nerve to actually phone an attorney and ask if she was really married to C.C. She had to be careful. It couldn't be a lawyer who knew her, so she called one in El Paso, giving the receptionist an assumed name. She was given an appointment for that afternoon, because the attorney had a cancellation in his busy schedule. She told the receptionist why she wanted to see the attorney, adding lightly that she'd gotten a Mexican marriage and thought it wasn't binding. The secretary laughed and said a lot of people thought that, only to find out to their astonishment that they were very binding in Texas. She reconfirmed the appointment, wished Pepi a nice day and hung up.

Pepi replaced the receiver with a dull thud and sat down heavily in the chair beside the telephone table in the hall. Her heart was beating madly. It would take having the lawyer look at the document to be sure, but it sounded as if his receptionist was right. Legally she was Mrs. C. C. Tremayne. She was Connal Tremayne's wife.

But he didn't know it.

The consequences of her deception could be far-reaching and tragic, especially if he decided to marry Edie. He would be commiting bigamy, and he wouldn't even know it.

What should she do? If she told him now, after having denied it when he'd demanded the truth, he'd never believe anything she said again. He'd hate her, too, for trapping him into marriage. It didn't matter that he'd threatened to land them in jail if she didn't go along. He'd been intoxicated, not responsible for his actions. But she'd been sober. When he asked her why she'd gone through with it, how would she answer him? Would he guess that she was shamefully in love with him?

The questions tormented her. She burned lunch. Her father gave her a hard glare as he bit into a scraped grilled cheese sandwich.

"Tastes like carbon," he muttered.

"Sorry." She'd forgotten to buy cheese at the store on her latest shopping trip, so there had been only enough for three sandwiches. She'd managed to burn all three. All she could do was scrape them off and hope for the best.

"You're been preoccupied all morning," he remarked with intense scrutiny of the bright color in her cheeks. "Want to talk about it?"

She managed a wan smile and shook her head. "Thanks anyway."

He got down another bite of overdone grilled cheese sandwich. "Would it have anything to do with C.C.'s absence last night?"

She stared at him blankly. "What?"

"C.C.'s car was missing all night, and I understand that he had to have one of the hands drive him over to Juárez to collect it this morning." He glared at the remainder of his sandwiches and pushed the plate away. "He was drinking, wasn't he, Pepi?"

She couldn't lie, but it wouldn't do to tell the truth, either. "One of the men said C.C. had a few in Juárez, but on his own time," she added quickly. "You can't really jump on him unless he does it on your time." She warmed to her subject. "Besides that, he only drinks once a year."

He frowned. "Once a year?"

"That's about the extent of it. And please don't ask me why, because I can't tell you." She laid a gentle hand on his forearm. "Dad, you know we owe the ranch to his business sense."

"I know," he muttered. "But damn it, Pepi, I can't have one set of rules for the men and another for him."

"He probably won't ever do it again," she said reassuringly. "Come on, you haven't actually caught him in the act, you know."

He grimaced. "I don't guess I have. But, if I ever do...!" he added hotly.

"I know. You'll throw him off the roof." She grinned. "Drink your coffee. At least it isn't burned." She finished hers. "I, uh, have to go into El Paso this afternoon to pick up a package I ordered."

He scowled. "What package?"

"For your birthday," she improvised. That wasn't improbable; his birthday was only two weeks away.

"What is it?" he asked.

"I'll never tell."

He let the subject drop after that, and went back out to work. Pepi washed up and then went to dress for her appointment. Jeans and a T-shirt weren't exactly the best outfit to wear to her own doom, she thought blackly.

She put on her full denim skirt with a blue print blouse and pinned her hair up on her head. She looked much more mature, she decided, although nothing could be done about the freckles on her nose. Not even makeup camouflaged them very well. She did the best she could, adding only a touch of makeup to her face and groaning over her voluptuous figure. If only she could lose enough weight to look like Edie...

With a moan, she slipped her hose-clad feet into taupe high heels, transferred the contents of her handbag into the pocketbook that matched the heels, and went downstairs.

As luck would have it, she ran right into C.C. on the front porch. He looked hung over and dusty. His batwing chaps were heavily stained, like the jeans under them and his chambray shirt. His hat had once been black, but now it was dusty gray. He glared down at her with black eyes.

"Brandon's out at the holding corral," he remarked in an oddly hostile tone. "I assume he's the reason for the fine feathers?"

"I'm going into El Paso to do some shopping," she replied. "How's your head?" Better to sound natural, she decided, and she even smiled.

"It was bad enough before I buried it in dust and bleating calves," he muttered. "Come in here a minute. I have to talk to you."

She knew her heart had stopped beating. With a sense of awe, she felt the warmth of his lean, strong hand around her upper arm as he guided her back into the house and shut the door. He let go of her almost reluctantly.

"Look, Pepi, this has got to stop," he said.

"W-what has?" she faltered.

"You chasing me down on my yearly binges," he said irritably. He took off his hat and ran a grimy hand through his sweaty jet hair. "I've been thinking all day about what could have happened to you in Juárez last night. That part of town is a rough place in broad daylight, never mind at night. I told you before, I don't need a nursemaid. I don't want you ever pulling such a stupid stunt again."

"There's a simple solution. Stop drinking," she said.

He searched her uplifted face quietly, scowling. "Yes, I think I might have to. If my memory's as faulty as it was last night . . ."

She had to exert every ounce of will she had not to give anything away. "Your secrets are safe with me, C.C.," she said in a stage whisper, and grinned.

He relaxed a little. "Okay, squirt. Go do your shopping." His dark eyes slid over her body in a way they never had before, and she felt her knees going weak.

"Something wrong?" she asked huskily.

His eyes caught hers. "You kick around in jeans so much that I forget occasionally that you've even got legs." His gaze dropped to them and he smiled in a sensual kind of way. "Very nice legs, at that."

She flushed. "My legs are none of your business, C.C.," she informed him.

He didn't like that. His sharp glance told her so. "Why? Do they belong to the carrot-topped vet already? He acts more like a lover than a friend, despite your constant denials." His expression seemed to harden before her eyes. "You're twenty-two, as you keep telling me. And this is a permissive age, isn't it? No man can expect virginity in a wife anymore."

The mention of the word "wife" made her face pale. But she couldn't let him see how shaken she was. "That's right," she said. "It is a permissive age. I can sleep with a man if I like."

He looked briefly murderous. "Does your father know about that attitude?"

"What my father doesn't know won't bother him," she said uneasily. "I have to go, C.C."

His eyes mirrored his contempt. "My God, I thought you were old-fashioned, in that respect at least."

That hurt. She lowered her gaze to his shirt. "As you keep telling me, my private life is no concern of yours," she said in a tight voice. "You and Edie probably don't play bingo on your dates, either, and I don't make nasty remarks about your morals."

"I'm a man," he said shortly.

She lifted her eyes defiantly. "So what? Do you think being a man gives you some divine right to sleep with anybody you like? If men expect chaste women, then women have the right to expect chaste men!"

His thick eyebrows lifted toward the ceiling. "My God, where would you find one?"

"That's my point exactly. Sling mud and it sticks to your fingers. Now I'm going."

"If you aren't meeting the handsome vet, who are you meeting, dressed like that?" he asked curtly.

"It's just a skirt and blouse!"

"Not the way you fill them out, little one," he said quietly. His eyes made emphatic statements about that before he lifted them back up to capture hers.

"I'm overweight," she got out.

"Really?" He pulled out a cigarette and lit it, but his eyes had hers in a stranglehold and he wouldn't let her avert her gaze.

Her heart raged in her chest, beating painfully hard and fast. Her lips parted on a shaky breath and she realized that her hands were clutching her purse so hard that her nails were leaving marks in the soft leather.

He moved closer, just close enough to threaten her with the warm strength of his body. He was so much taller that she had to look up to see his eyes, but she couldn't manage to tear her gaze away.

The back of his forefinger touched her cheek in a slow, devastating caress. "I thought you were a total innocent, little Pepi," he said, his voice at least an octave deeper. "If that's not the case, you could find yourself in over your head very quickly."

Her lips parted. She was drowning in him, so intoxicated that she didn't even mind the smell of calf and burned hide that clung to him. Her eyes fell to his hard mouth, to its thin chiseled lines, and she wanted it with a primitive hunger. It occurred to her that she could entice him into her bed, that she could sleep with him. They were legally married, even if he didn't know it. She could seduce him. The delicious thought made her breath catch.

Then came the not-so-delicious thought of what would happen afterward. With the experience she was pretty sure he had, he might know that she was virginal, by her reactions if nothing else. Besides that, it might hurt, which would be a dead giveaway. And he didn't know they were married. All sorts of complications could arise. No, she thought miserably, she couldn't even have that consolation. Not even one night to hold in her memory. She had to keep him at arm's length until she could decide how to tell him the truth and what to do about it.

She backed away a little, forcing a smile. "I really have to go," she said huskily. "See you later."

He muttered something under his breath and opened the door for her, his dark eyes accusing as they watched her go. She was getting under his skin. It made him angry that her body enticed him, that he was hungry for her. It made him angrier that she was apparently experienced. He didn't want other hands touching her, especially the vet's. She'd been his caretaker for so long now that he'd come to look upon her with the same passion a wine maker felt for his best vintage. But he'd thought she was virginal, and she'd as good as told him she wasn't. That realization changed everything. He'd placed her carefully off limits for years, but if she wasn't innocent, then he didn't have to worry about his conscience. Odd, though, he thought as he watched her go, she could still blush prettily enough when he looked at her body. Maybe she wasn't very experienced, despite the redheaded veterinarian's attentions. C.C.'s black eyes narrowed. Brandon didn't have his experience, so that gave him an edge. Yes, it did. He lifted the cigarette to his mouth and smiled faintly as he watched Pepi climb into her father's old Lincoln and drive away.

Blissfully unaware of C.C.'s plotting, Pepi managed to get the car out of the driveway without hitting anything. Her hands on the steering wheel were still shaking from her unexpected confrontation. That was the first time that C.C. had ever made anything resembling a pass at her. Perhaps she should have been less emphatic about her experience—of which she didn't have any. But she'd felt threatened by the way C.C. had looked at her, and her mind had shut down. For one long second she agonized over the thought that he might take her off the endangered species list and start pursuing her himself. But, no, he had Edie to satisfy those needs. He wouldn't want an innocent like herself. And then she remembered that

she'd told him she was no innocent. What would she do
if he made a heavy pass at her? She loved him to distrac-
tion, but she didn't dare let things go that far. If the worst
came to pass and they were really married, she could get
an annulment without much difficulty. But if she admit-
ted him to her bed, it would mean getting a divorce, and
that would take much longer. She couldn't afford to give
in to temptation, no matter how appealing it was. . . .

The attorney's office was located adjacent to a new
shopping center that had just opened on the outskirts of
town. She pulled into a parking spot in front of the adobe
facade of the office building and took a deep breath. This
wasn't going to be very pleasant, she was afraid.

She went in and produced the document. The attorney
took his time looking it over. He was bilingual, so the
wording that had sent Pepi crazy trying to decipher with
the help of a Spanish-English dictionary made perfect
sense to him.

"It's legal, I assure you," he mused, handing it back.
"Congratulations," he added with a smile.

"He doesn't know we're married." She groaned. She
told him the particulars. "Doesn't that mean anything,
that he was intoxicated?"

"If he was sober enough to agree to be married, to in-
itiate the ceremony and to sign his name to a legal certi-
ficate of marriage," he said, "I'm afraid it is binding."

"Then I'll just have to get an annulment," she said
heavily.

"No problem," he said, smiling again. "Just have him
come in and sign—"

"He has to know about it!" she exclaimed, horrified.

"I'm afraid so," he said. "Even if he did apparently get married without realizing it, there's just no way the marriage can be dissolved without his consent."

Pepi buried her face in her hands. "I can't tell him. I just can't!"

"You really have to," he said. "There are all kinds of legal complications that this could create. If he's a reasonable man, surely he'll understand."

"Oh, no, he won't," she said on a miserable sigh. "But you're right. I do have to tell him. And I will," she added, rising to shake his hand. She didn't say when.

Pepi mentally flayed herself for not telling C.C. the truth when he'd demanded it. She'd only wanted to spare him embarrassment, and she hadn't thought any damage would be done. Besides that, the thought of being his wife, just for a little while, was so sweet a temptation that she hadn't been able to resist. Now she was stuck with the reality of her irresponsibility, and she didn't know what she was going to do.

For a start, she avoided C.C. With roundup in full swing, and the men working from dawn until long after dark, that wasn't too hard. She spent her own free time with Brandon, wishing secretly that she could feel for him what she felt for C.C. Brandon was so much fun, and they were compatible. It was just that there was no spark of awareness between them.

"I wish you wouldn't spend so much time with Hale," her father said at supper one night near the end of the massive roundup, during one of his rare evenings at home.

"There, there, you're just jealous because he's getting all your apple pies while you're out working," she teased.

He sighed. "No, it's not that at all. I want to see you in a happy marriage, girl. The kind your mother and I had. Hale's a fine young man, but he's too biddable. You'd be leading him around by the nose by the end of your first year together. You're feisty, like your mother. You need a man who can stand up to you, a man you can't dominate.''

Only one man came immediately to mind and she flushed, averting her eyes. "The one you're thinking of is already spoken for," she said tersely.

His eyes, so much like her own, searched her face. "Pepi, you're old enough now to understand why men see women like Edie. He's a man. He has...a man's needs.''

She picked up her fork and looked at it, trying not to feel any more uncomfortable than she already did. "Edie is his business, as he once told me. We have no right to interfere in his private life.''

"She's an odd choice for a ranch foreman, isn't she?" he mused, still watching her like a hawk. "A city sophisticate, a divorcée, a woman used to wealth and position. Don't you find it unexpected that she likes C.C.?''

"Not really. He's quite sophisticated himself," she reminded him. "He seems to fit in anywhere. Even at business conferences," she added, recalling a conference the three of them had attended two years ago. She and her father had both been surprised at the sight of C.C. in a dinner jacket talking stocks and bonds and investments with a rancher over cocktails. It had been an eye-opening experience for Pepi.

"Yes, I remember," her father agreed. "A mysterious man, C.C. He came out of nowhere, literally. I've never been able to find out anything about his background. But from time to time, things slip out. He's not a man unused to wealth and position, and at times he makes me feel like a rank beginner in business. He can manipulate stocks with the best of them. It was his expertise that helped me put the ranch into the black. Not to mention those new techniques in cattle management that he bulldozed me into trying. Embryo transplants, artificial insemination, hormone implants...although he and I mutually decided to stop the hormone implants. There's been a lot of negative talk about it among consumers."

"Negative talk never stopped C.C.," she said, chuckling.

"True enough, but he thinks like I do about it. If implants cut back beef consumption because people are afraid of the hormones, that cuts our profits."

"I give up," she said, holding up both hands. "Put away your shooting irons."

"Sorry," he murmured, and smiled back.

"Actually I agree with you," she confessed. "I just like to hear you hold forth. I'm going dancing with Brandon on Friday night. Okay?"

He looked reluctant, but he didn't argue. "Okay, as long as you remember that my birthday's Saturday night and you're going out with me."

"Yes, sir. As if I could forget. Thirty-nine, isn't it...?"

"Shut up and carve that apple pie," he said, gesturing toward it.

"Whatever you say."

She tried not to think about C.C. for the rest of the week, but it was impossible not to catch an occasional glimpse of him in the saddle, going from one corral to the next. He let the herd representatives ride in the Jeep— representatives from other ranches in the area checking brands to make sure that none of their cattle had crossed into Mathews territory. It was a common courtesy locally, because of the vast territory the ranches in south Texas covered. Her father ran over two thousand head of cattle, and when they threw calves, it took some effort to get them all branded, tattooed, ear-tagged and vaccinated each spring and fall. It was a dirty, hot, thankless chore that caused occasional would-be cowboys to quit and go back to working in textile plants and furniture shops. Cowboying, while romantic and glamorous to the unknowing, was low paying, backbreaking and prematurely aging as a profession. It meant living with the smell of cow chips, burning hide, leather and dirt—long hours in the saddle, long hours of fixing machinery and water pumps and vehicles and doctoring sick cattle. There was a television in the bunkhouse, but hardly ever any time to watch it except late on summer evenings. Ranch work was year-round with few lazy periods, because there was always something that needed doing.

The advantages of the job were freedom, freedom, and freedom. A man lived close to the earth. He had time to watch the skies and feel the urgent rhythm of life all around him. He lived as man perhaps was meant to live, without technology strangling his mind, without the smells and pressures of civilization to cripple his spirit. He was one with nature, with life itself. He didn't answer to an alarm clock or some corporation's image of what a businessman should be. He might not make a lot of money, he might risk life and limb daily, but he was as free as a modern man could get. If he did his job well and carefully, he had job security for all his life.

Pepi thought about that, and decided that it might not be such a bad thing after all, being a cowboy. But the title and job description, while it might fit C.C., sat oddly on his broad shoulders. He was much too sophisticated to look at home in dirty denims. It was easier now to picture him in a dinner jacket. All the same, he did look fantastic in the saddle, riding a horse as easily as if he'd been born on one. He was long and lean and graceful, even in a full gallop, and she'd seen him break a horse to saddle more than once. It was a treat to watch. He never hurt the horse's spirit in the process, but once he was on its back, there was never any doubt about who the master was. He stuck like glue, his hard face taut with strain, his eyes glittering, his thin lips smiling savagely with the effort as he rode the animal to submission.

The picture stuck in Pepi's mind, and brought with it disturbing sensations of another kind of conquest. She was no prude, and despite her innocence, she knew what men and woman did together in bed. But the sensation, the actual feelings they shared were alien to her. She wondered if C.C. would be like that in bed, if he'd have that same glittery look in his eyes, that same savage smile on his thin lips as he brought a woman to ecstasy under the driving force of his hard, sweat-glistened body...

She went scarlet. Fortunately there was nobody nearby to see her. She darted into the house and up the staircase to get dressed for her dinner date with Brandon.

They went to a restaurant in downtown El Paso, one famous in the area for the size of its steaks and for its view of the city at night from its fourteenth-floor location in a well-known hotel.

"I do love the view from up here," Pepi told Brandon, smiling at him as they were shown to a seat by the huge windows overlooking the Franklin Mountains. The Franklins, in fact, were responsible for the city's name, because the pass that separated the Franklins from the Juárez Mountains to the south was called *El Paso del Norte*—the path of the north. Part of the mountain chain was located in the city of El Paso itself. The only major desert city in Texas, El Paso shared much history with Mexico's Juárez, across the border. Pancho Villa lived in

El Paso after his exile from his own country, and historically the Texas city, which sat on the Butterfield Overland stage route in the late nineteenth century had been the site of Indian attacks and a replica of old Fort Bliss marked the former home of the cavalry that once fought the Apaches, including the famous Chief Victorio. Modern day Fort Bliss was the home of the largest air defense center of the free world. Not far from the restaurant where Pepi and Brandon were eating was the Acme Saloon, where gunfighter John Wesley Hardin was shot in the back and killed.

On a less grim note, there was an aerial tramway up to Ranger Peak, giving tourists a view of seven thousand square miles of mountain and desert. There were one hundred parks in El Paso, not to mention museums, old missions, and plenty of attractions across the border in Mexico's largest border city, Juárez.

Pepi had lived near El Paso all her life, and she had the love of the desert that comes from living near it. Tourists might see an expanse of open land nestled between mountain ranges with no apparent life. Pepi saw flowering agave and prickly pear cactus, stately organ pipe cactus and creosote bushes, graceful mesquite trees and the wonder of the mountain ranges at sunset. She loved the desert surrounding the city. Of course, she loved her own home more. The land down near Fort Hancock where the ranch was located was just a bit more hospitable than this, and her roots were there.

"The view from up here is pretty great," Brandon agreed, drawing her out of her reveries. "But you suit me better than the desert and the mountains," he added, his gaze approving her simple mauve dress with its crystal pleats and cap sleeves. Her hair, in an elegant bun, drew attention to the exquisite lines of her face and the size of her pale brown eyes. She'd used more makeup than usual and she looked honestly pretty, freckles and all. But it was her figure that held Brandon's attention. When she dressed up, she was dynamite.

"What will you have to drink?" the waitress asked with a smile, diverting both of them.

"Just white wine for me," Pepi replied.

"I'll have the same," her escort added.

The waitress left and Brandon, resplendent in a dark suit, leaned his forearms on the spotless white tablecloth and stared at her warmly. "Why won't you marry me?" he asked. "Does it have something to do with the fact that I hang out with animals?"

She laughed. "I love animals. But I'm not quite ready for marriage yet." Then she remembered that she *was* married, and her heart dropped. She shifted back in her chair, feeling vaguely guilty at being out with Brandon when she was legally another man's wife. Of course, the man she was married to didn't know it. That made her feel a little better, at least.

"You're an old lady of twenty-two," he persisted. "You'll be over the hill before you know it."

"No, I won't. I haven't even decided what I want to do with my life yet." That was true. She'd never gone to college. Somehow, after she'd graduated from high school, there had been too much to demand her time at home. "I like figures," she murmured absently. "I thought I might take an accounting course or something."

"You could come and work for me. I need a book-keeper," he said instantly.

"Sorry, but so does Dad. Jack Berry, our present bookkeeper, is hopeless. So is Dad. If I decide to take on bookkeeping, you'd better believe that Dad will scoop me up first. He hates having to redo Jack's figuring.''

"I guess . . . Well, well, look at that dress!''

It was unusual for Brandon to be so wickedly interested in what any woman wore. Pepi turned her head slightly to follow his gaze and her heart froze in her chest.

Edie was just coming in the door, wearing a red dress that was cut to the waist in back and dipped in a faintly low V in front. Despite its length, it was an advertisement for her blond beauty, and she drew eyes. Just behind her stood a bored-looking C.C. in a dark vested suit, his hard face showing lines of tiredness from the two weeks of work he'd just put in. Pepi could hardly bear to look at him.

He must have felt her stare because his head turned and even across the room she registered the impact of that level look. She averted her eyes and smiled at Brandon.

"You might as well keep your leering looks to yourself,'' she said more pleasantly than she wanted to. "C.C.'s pretty possessive of her.''

"He's giving you a hard glare. Were you supposed to stay home tonight or something?''

"No. He's probably just tired,'' she emphasized, trying not to remember the last face-to-face confrontation she'd had with her father's foreman. It made her pulse leap and catch fire just to think about the way he'd talked to her, the things he'd said. She loved everything about him, but if his attentiveness to Edie was anything to go by, the feeling was hardly mutual. She carefully avoided glancing at him again, oblivious to his angry scowl and preoccupied manner while he ate his own supper.

Chapter Four

If Pepi had hoped that C.C. and his girlfriend would leave without saying anything, she was doomed to disappointment. After he and Edie had finished dessert, he went straight to Pepi's table, dragging the unwilling blonde along with him.

"Well, hello," Brandon said, smiling at them. "How does it feel to finally be through with roundup, C.C.? I'm royally sick of it myself, and I've still got two herds to examine tomorrow."

"It's nice to have a little free time," the older man said quietly. His black eyes were carving up Pepi's face. "I haven't laid eyes on you for two weeks," he told her curtly. "I wondered if you've been avoiding me."

Pepi was shocked by the sudden attack, as well as by the venom in his deep voice. She wasn't the only one. Brandon and Edie exchanged questioning glances, too.

"I haven't been avoiding you," Pepi said, but she couldn't quite meet those eyes with the memory of their last confrontation between them. "You've been out with the men all day and most of the night, just like Dad. I've had things of my own to do, keeping up with the cooking and helping Wiley organize supplies for the chuck wagon."

The Bar M was one of the few ranches that still operated a chuck wagon. The ranch was so big that it wasn't practical to have two dozen men trucking back and forth to the bunkhouse kitchen to be fed. Wiley, one of the older hands, cooked and Pepi helped him keep supplies in.

"You usually come out and watch us work," C.C. persisted, his eyes narrowing.

It was a question, and Pepi didn't want to answer it. She tangled her fingers in her napkin, vaguely aware of Edie's frown as she watched the byplay.

"I'm overweight," Pepi told him belligerently, glaring up at him. "All right? I find it hard to get in the saddle these days. Now are you satisfied!"

"You're not overweight," C.C. said shortly.

"She is, a bit," Edie murmured apologetically, taking C.C.'s arm possessively. "We girls are sensitive about those extra pounds, aren't we, Penelope?" she added with a dry laugh. "Especially when it lands around our hips."

What hips? Pepi wanted to ask, because Edie looked more like a bean pole than a woman with her exaggerated thinness. The older woman's comments had hurt, and Pepi wished she knew why she'd ever brought the subject up in the first place. It had been clumsy and stupid; her usual condition when C.C. came close these days.

"I think Pepi's just right," Brandon murmured, smiling reassuringly at her. "She suits me."

"You angel," Pepi said, smiling at him.

"Why isn't your father with you?" C.C. asked suddenly, his face gone hard at the way Pepi was smiling at the redheaded vet.

Pepi started, her big eyes gaping up at him as if she feared for his sanity. "I don't usually take my father on dates, C.C.," she said.

"Tomorrow is his birthday," he reminded her with faint sarcasm, bristling with bad humor. He hated seeing her with Hale, hated having her avoid him. He felt that it was probably the things he'd said to her that had sent her running, but deeper still was resentment that she was more than likely sleeping with that clown next to her. The thought of Pepi in another man's bed drove him out of his mind. He'd been short-tempered and unapproachable almost the whole time he was working roundup because of the casual way she'd denied being innocent. God knew how many dreams he'd had about relieving her of that condition, and in the most tender way. Now his illusions were shattered, and he wanted to make her as miserable as she'd made him.

"I know tomorrow is his birthday." Pepi faltered. "Brandon and I are taking him to the *Diez Y Seis de Septiembre* parade in the morning. Aren't we, Brandon?" she added, almost frantic. They weren't taking her father anywhere, but she couldn't bear to tell C.C. that all she'd planned was a birthday cake and a nice supper. Not when he was looking at her as if she were public enemy number one and the most ungrateful daughter on earth.

"That's right," Brandon agreed immediately.

Hale, again, C.C. thought furiously. He lifted his chin and looked down his straight nose at her. He spared

Brandon a cold, barely civil glance. "I suppose he'll be grateful that you bothered about his birthday."

"What in the world's come over you?" Pepi asked defensively. Was he trying to start a fight, for heaven's sake? She stiffened in her chair, aware of Edie's surprised scrutiny of her escort.

"He's had a hard couple of weeks, that's what," Brandon said with a forced smile, trying to relieve the tension. "I ought to know. I've been out there most days."

"Roundup makes everybody bad-tempered," Pepi agreed. She looked up at Edie. "How are you? I love your dress."

"This old rag?" Edie chuckled. "Thanks. I thought it might cheer up my friend here, but it hasn't seemed to do much for him."

"Oh, hasn't it?" C.C. murmured, diverted at last. He glanced briefly at Pepi before he slid a possessive arm around Edie's shoulders and pulled her close, his eyes warm, his voice deep and sensuous. "Come along, and I'll see if I can't convince you that it has."

"Now there's an offer I won't refuse," Edie murmured huskily. "Good night, Penelope, Brandon."

They murmured their farewells and Pepi refused to watch them walk away. He was her husband. She wanted to stand up and shout it, to drag Edie away from him. They were going off somewhere to be alone, and she knew what would happen; she could see it in her mind. She ground her teeth together.

"Poor thing," Brandon said then, his blue eyes full of concern and sudden understanding. "So that's how it is."

"I've been looking out for him for a long time," Pepi said defensively. "I'm overly protective. I have to stop it.

He's not my chick, and I'm not his mother hen. Well, maybe once a year, but only then."

Brandon wasn't buying it. He covered her hand on the table with his own. "If you ever need a shoulder to cry on, you can use mine," he said gently. "And if you ever get over him..."

"Thanks," she said, forcing a smile.

"I guess you know that I can't take you and your father to the parade in the morning?" he added.

She nodded, smiling. "Sorry. I don't even know why I said it. He made me mad. I was going to bake my father a cake, that's all."

"I wouldn't mind helping him eat it, but I'm going to be out all day tomorrow with old man Reynolds's herd," he said ruefully. "I won't be home until after midnight, more than likely."

"I'll save you a piece of cake. Thanks for pulling my irons out of the fire."

"You're welcome." He frowned. "It's not like C.C. to start fights with you in public. Odd that he'd take you to task over your dad."

She couldn't tell him that C.C. had been spoiling for a fight ever since she'd gone overboard and lied about her maidenly condition. Anyway, it didn't matter. C.C.'s opinion didn't bother her. Not one bit!

"Maybe he's just frustrated because he's been away from Edie for two weeks," she said miserably and felt her heart breaking at the thought of how much lost time he could make up for tonight with his blond attachment....

She felt sick. "It's ever so complicated, Brandon," she sighed. "I've managed to get us into a terrible mess, and, no, I can't talk about it. Can we go, please? I've got a headache."

He took her home and she managed to get away without a good-night kiss. C.C.'s appearance had ruined the evening for her. She'd hoped to keep him out of her mind for a little while, but fate seemed to have other ideas.

She hardly slept. She got up with a dull headache and it got worse when C.C. came in smiling and looking like a hungry cat with canary feathers sticking out both sides of his mouth. She didn't need a scorecard to know why he was so smug and content. He'd probably had a hell of a sweet night with Edie, but while she'd always suspected what his relationship with the blonde actually was, her feelings overwhelmed her. She glared at C.C. with eyes that almost hated him, her freckles standing out in a pale, haunted face.

"What do you want?" she demanded testily.

His eyebrows arched. "Coffee, for now. And a word with your father before you and the happy vet take him off to town."

She'd told a bald-faced lie the night before, and now she was standing in the middle of it with nothing to say. Her face slowly flamed scarlet.

His black eyes narrowed. He pushed back the brim of his Stetson and leaned against the kitchen counter, his blue striped Western shirt complementing the darkness of his face and hair and eyes, his powerful leg muscles rippling under tight denims as he shifted his position.

"Are you taking him to the parade?" he asked, his tone less belligerent than it had been the night before.

She shook her head, wiping flour off her hands and dabbing at a streak of it on the denim skirt that she was wearing with a yellow tank top.

"Why did you say you were?" he added.

She glanced at him angrily. "Because you made me sound like a female Jack the Ripper last night, as if I didn't even care about my own father."

His eyes slid down her body and back up again, a visual touch that made her nerves sit up and scream. No man had ever looked at her like that, so sensually that she felt as if he'd stroked her bare breasts. She caught her breath.

He trapped her eyes with his, reading her response in them. So she wasn't immune to him. She might be experienced, but she was vulnerable just the same. A faint smile touched his hard mouth.

"I know you care about your father," he said. "I just don't like the amount of time you spend with Hale."

"Brandon is—"

"A clown," he finished for her, his smile fading. "Too irresponsible and flighty for a woman with your depth. He's probably never satisfied you once."

What he meant was evident in his tone, and she almost dropped the bag of flour in her haste to put it away. She kept her back to him while she made biscuits, hoping he'd go away.

"He makes me laugh," she said through her teeth.

He came up behind her, his body so close that she could feel the heat and strength of it at her back, smell the faint cologne he wore. She tensed all over, waiting for him to touch her, waiting for his lean hands to bite into her waist and jerk her back into his body, for those same hands to smooth up her rib cage to her full, throbbing breasts and cup them. . . .

"What are you doing?" he asked.

Her eyes blinked. He wasn't touching her. She felt his breath on her nape, but he was just looking over her shoulder, that was all. But she was on fire to kiss his hard mouth, to touch him, to hold him against her. She had to clench her teeth to still the feverish excitement he created with his proximity. Perhaps he didn't realize how vulnerable she was, and she wanted to keep it that way.

"I'm making biscuits." Heavens, was that husky whisper really her voice?

"And ham? I like country ham."

"Yes, I know. I'm going to fry it while the biscuits cook. There's coffee on the stove if you want some."

"I noticed."

But he didn't move. She started pinching off biscuits and laying them neatly into the round baking pan in front of her, but her hands were trembling. He was tormenting her. She wanted to scream.

She turned her head helplessly and looked up into his eyes, and all at once she knew. That flicker of mocking amusement in his face was enough to convince her that he was all too aware of the effect he had on her.

"Do I bother you, Pepi?" he drawled, deliberately letting his gaze drop to her full, parted lips. "Surely I shouldn't if Hale is enough for you."

Her breath was ragged. She forced her head back down so that she could concentrate on her biscuits. "Is Edie enough for you?" she countered outrageously.

"When I'm in the mood, anything with breasts is enough for me," he said curtly, angered by her refusal to admit her interest in him.

"C.C.!" she burst out, whirling.

His hands slid past her wide hips to rest on either side of her on the table, effectively trapping her. His gaze was relentlessly probing. "You don't want me to know that you're attracted to me. Why?"

"This isn't fair," she whispered. "I've looked out for you for years, I've done my best to make you comfortable, to help you when I could. Is this any way to pay me back for being your friend?''

He stared at her unblinkingly. "I told you, I don't need a nursemaid. But you've been avoiding me and I don't like it. I want to know why."

"And this is how you plan to find out?" she asked, her voice wobbling a little, because his nearness was devastating to her senses.

"It's the quickest way," he replied. "You've been backing away ever since that day in the hall." His eyes narrowed to glittering slits. "In fact, you've been backing away since that night in Juárez. What did I do to you, Pepi? Did I try to make love to you?"

"No!" she burst out.

"Then what happened?" he asked.

She couldn't tell him. She should, but she couldn't. She lowered her eyes to his broad chest. "You said I could probably throw you over my shoulder and carry you out of the bar," she said dully, repeating the blistering insult he'd thrown at her. "That I was nothing but a tomboy. . ."

He didn't remember. But he could see the hurt on her face, and that disturbed him. "I was drinking," he said gently. "You know I didn't mean anything I said."

She laughed painfully. "No? I thought people always told the truth when they drank, because they were uninhibited."

He drew in a slow, deep breath. "What else did I say?"

"That was more than enough. I closed my ears to the rest of it."

"And that's why you've been avoiding me?" he persisted, as if it mattered. In fact, it did. He'd been smarting ever since, hurt by her avoidance as he'd rarely been hurt by anything.

She hesitated. Then she nodded.

He bent his head and laid his cheek against hers, nuzzling it gently. The silence in the kitchen grew hot with restrained excitement. She could almost hear her own heartbeat...or was it his? She all but stopped breathing. He smelled of cologne and tobacco, and his cheek was rough and warm where it lay against hers. He didn't try to kiss her, or even pull her against him. But his face drew slowly against her own, and she felt his thick eyelashes against her cheek, her chin, her soft throat, felt the heat of his tobacco-scented breath on her breasts as his forehead rested on her collarbone and she felt the bridge of his nose on the bare swell of her breast where it slowly pushed the fabric out of the way....

"Pepi, where the hell is the newspaper?"

C.C. lifted his head as her father's voice exploded from the hall. He stared down at her shocked face with narrowed eyes in a face like honed steel. He edged away from the table, his lean hands at his sides, and his gaze dropped to the drooping neckline of the tank top, which her cold fingers fumbled to adjust.

She met C.C.'s gaze for one long, shattering instant and then she turned abruptly back to her biscuits with trembling hands and a heartbeat that shook her.

"There you are. Morning, C.C.," her father said with a chuckle. "I found the paper," he added, waving it as he went to the table and sat down. "Pepi had already brought it in."

"Happy Birthday," Pepi said with a forced smile. "I'm making breakfast."

"So I noticed. Do I get a cake?"

"Coconut, your favorite, and all your favorite foods for supper," she added.

"C.C., you can come over and help me eat it," he told the younger man.

"I'm afraid not," C.C. replied, glancing at Pepi's rigid spine. "I'm taking Edie to the parade, and then down to Juárez to spend the day shopping."

"Well, you'll enjoy that, I'm sure," Ben said slowly, aware of odd undercurrents in the kitchen.

"Come with us. You, too, Pepi," he added carelessly. "We'll celebrate your birthday in Mexico," he told Ben.

"Great idea! I haven't taken a day off since I don't know when. Pepi will enjoy it, too. We'll do it, then tonight you and Edie can come home with us and have supper, can't they, Pepi?"

She was going to die. She knew she was going to die. Thank God nobody could see her face. "Of course they can," she said through her teeth. "We'll have a lovely time." What else could she say, she wondered. After all, it was Ben's birthday. He was entitled to spend it the way he pleased. But she was still going up in flames at the way C.C. had touched her, and the thought of watching him with Edie all day made her want to run screaming into the yard.

"Just the four of us," C.C. added as he sat down with a cup of coffee in his hand. "Not Hale."

She swallowed. "Brandon can't come anyway. He's going to be working all day and most of the night."

"I thought you liked Brandon," Ben Mathews remarked, eyeing C.C. curiously.

"I do. I just don't like him hanging around Pepi," C.C. replied honestly. He glanced at her rigid back and away. "She can do better."

Ben chuckled. Now the undercurrents began to make sense. He shot a curious look toward his daughter, not missing the flush on her cheeks and the way she fumbled biscuits into the oven. He wondered for a minute what he'd interrupted by bursting into the kitchen. Then C.C. asked him a question about the culled cattle he was selling off, and the moment was forgotten.

The biscuits went fast. Pepi had to grab to get one at all, and the ham and scrambled eggs went even faster.

"You're inhaling it!" she accused them.

"Can I help it if you're the best cook around?" C.C. asked innocently.

"A good cook beats a fashion plate any day," her father remarked bluntly. "Ought to marry this girl, C.C., before she takes her pots and pans elsewhere."

"Dad!" Pepi exclaimed, shattered. She went white with horror, remembering that marriage license in her bureau drawer.

C.C. frowned. That was an odd reaction for a woman who'd been as responsive as she had a few minutes ago. She was acting pretty oddly lately, and he didn't believe it was only because he'd hurt her feelings in Juárez. No, there had to be something more. Something had happened that night, he was sure of it. But what?

"I don't want to get married, to a good cook or a fashion plate," he murmured absently to Ben, scowling as he turned his attention back to the biscuit he was buttering. He missed the expression on Pepi's face.

"Don't you want kids?" Ben asked curiously.

Pepi could have cried when she saw the way that innocent question affected C.C. Her father didn't know what she did about their foreman's past.

"Have another biscuit," she broke in, shoving the plate in her father's face with a scowl.

He was quick, was Ben. He realized instantly that he'd said something he shouldn't. "Well, where's the honey?"

he demanded, camouflaging the brief silence. "You've eaten it all, haven't you? It was my honey!"

"It was your apple pie," she threw back. "You ate every bit of it and didn't even offer me any, so you can forget the honey, it's mine!" She clutched the jar to her breasts and glared at him across the table.

C.C. was touched by her attempt to protect him, even now. He watched her quietly, thinking how attractive she was, extra pounds and all. Come to think of it, she didn't look overweight. She looked just as a woman should, all soft and rounded and sweet. He liked her freckles and the way her hair caught fire and burned like bronze and honey in the sun. He liked the way she talked, the way she smelled. He liked a lot of things about her. And if it hadn't been for the tormenting memories, for the wounds of the past, he might have considered marrying her. But no, marriage wasn't something he coveted. It was a part of life he'd already experienced. Despite his jealousy of Hale, the other man would probably be better for Pepi than he would.

He never should have touched her. Now he was going to have to undo the damage he'd just done by losing his head before Ben walked in. He'd have to play up to Edie to throw Pepi off the track, to make sure she didn't get any ideas about him. Friendship was all he had to offer, and the sooner he made that clear to her the better. But he was going to have to keep his emotions under control to accomplish that. She went to his head, more so every day. He'd said and done things that he'd never meant to; he'd deliberately made passes at her. He couldn't understand his loss of control, or his sudden fascination with Pepi. Perhaps the long hours and hard work of the past few weeks were telling on him. He frowned and studied his cooling coffee. Maybe what he needed was a vacation. God knew he hadn't taken one in three years. He might go back to Jacobsville, Texas, where he was born, and visit his three brothers who were running the family business in his absence. He might go and try to face the past, if he could.

"I said, when do you want to leave?" Ben asked him for the second time.

"About nine-thirty," he said, tossing down the rest of his coffee. "We don't want to get there too late for the parade."

"Are you sure you want both of us along?" Pepi asked hesitantly.

He got up and glared at her. "It's your father's birthday. Of course I'm sure. Edie and I will enjoy having company." His eyes narrowed. "After all, we're alone most of the time. As we will be tonight, when I take her home. I don't mind sharing her occasionally."

Ben chuckled, but Pepi felt as if she'd been slapped. Coming so close on the heels of C.C.'s ardor, it was painful to be reminded that he belonged to someone else. She got up and began to clear the table absently.

C.C. went out the door without looking back. He hated hurting her. He never should have touched her.

Pepi took her time dressing. She'd thought about wearing one of her colorful Mexican dresses for the parade, with their lavish embroidery so delicate against the bone-white cotton and lace. But if Edie was going along, she might as well not bother to look feminine. Beside the blonde, she felt like an oversized tank.

She put on gray slacks and a bulky khaki top, tying her hair back in a severe ponytail. She looked terrible, she thought as she saw her reflection, defiantly leaving off makeup as well. Good. That would show C.C. Tremayne what she thought of him!

It did. He scowled at the sight of her, no less than her father had when she'd come downstairs.

"What the hell happened to you?" C.C. demanded. He'd changed, too, into a very becoming yellow knit designer shirt and tan slacks, a creamy Stetson perched on his black hair.

"What do you mean? I look the way I always do," Pepi defended.

"You didn't look like that last night," he said accusingly.

"Last night, I dressed up for Brandon," she said, staring back at him. "You have Edie to dress up for you," she added meaningfully.

C.C. shifted his eyes uncomfortably. He'd deserved that. "Ready to go, Ben?" he asked the older man, who was dressed casually himself.

"Just let me get my hat." He glanced at his daughter and scowled. "You could have worn that Mexican dress, just for me. I thought it looked just right for a fiesta."

"It doesn't fit," she lied, averting her gaze from C.C. "Besides, I look like a hippo in it...."

"You don't look like a hippo," C.C. said angrily. "My God, will you stop harping on your weight? You're just right. At least you look like a woman. People don't have to stop and guess when you walk by!"

Pepi stared at him with raised eyebrows. He glared at her and turned away just as Ben joined them.

She wondered if she was ever going to understand him. He was acting so completely erratic these days, like a man in love. She sighed. Probably it was just a matter of time before he and Edie tied the knot, despite what he'd said at the breakfast table about not wanting to marry again. She turned, picking up her purse on the way out the door.

Anyway, why would he look twice at her with someone as beautiful as Edie on his arm?

Edie was waiting in C.C.'s Ford, looking bored and irritable.

"Finally!" she muttered. "It's hot out here!"

"Sorry. I had to find my hat," Ben mumbled as he put Pepi into the back seat and climbed in beside her.

"I didn't mean to sound like that, Ben," Edie purred, all smiles when C.C. climbed in under the wheel and cranked the car. "You know we're delighted to have you, and Pepi, with us today. Happy Birthday!"

"Thanks," Ben said. He glanced at his daughter's quiet, sad face. She sat stiffly beside him, staring blankly out the window. He was beginning to get the picture about the way she felt. If she wasn't in love with C.C., she was giving a good imitation of a woman who was.

"Well, on to the parade," Edie mused, checking her makeup in her compact mirror. "Want to borrow a lipstick, Pepi? I didn't realize I'd rushed C.C. that much."

"I'm not wearing any," Pepi replied, "but thank you."

Edie glanced at her and then shrugged.

The parade was colorful and there was a crowd. The *Diez Y Seis de Septiembre* celebration was the annual observance of Mexico's independence from Spain— Mexico's Independence Day. Pepi always enjoyed the music and the floats, and the carnival atmosphere, but today she was preoccupied. She put on a happy face for her father's benefit, hoping he wouldn't see through it. But C.C.'s obvious interest in Edie was killing her. He had a possessive arm around the blonde, and once he bent and kissed her hungrily in full view of Pepi and the rest of El Paso.

Pepi turned away to buy a pinwheel from a passing vendor, glad for the diversion. She handed it to her father, deliberately keeping her eyes away from C.C.

"Happy Birthday, Dad," she said gently and smiled. "I've got your present at home. I thought you could have it with your cake after supper."

"That will be a nice touch." He patted her shoulder. "Sorry about this," he murmured, nodding toward an oblivious C.C. and Edie. "I should have refused."

"No, you shouldn't. It's your birthday." She smiled. "It's for the best, you know. I was wearing my heart out on him. It's just as well that I have to face how he really feels. Dreams are sweet, but you can't build a future on them."

"You've been different lately, Pepi," her father said surprisingly. "Is there anything you want to tell me?"

"A lot." She turned her eyes toward C.C. "But, first I have to tell him something. I should have told him before, but it's not too late. The minute we get home I'll make it all right. Then," she said with a rueful smile, "I'm going to need a shoulder to cry on, I think."

"You aren't in trouble, or anything?" her father asked hesitantly.

She laughed. "Not the kind you're thinking, no." She sighed and watched the parade. "It will be all right," she said, trying to convince herself. "It's just a little thing. Just a minor inconvenience."

She hoped C.C. would see it like that. She had to tell him today, before she lost her nerve. He and Edie were getting involved, anybody could see that. She couldn't, in all good conscience, let him face a bigamy charge because of her own stubborn pride. Tonight, she'd tell him the truth, and hope for the best.

Chapter Five

They went past the border guards for the day trip into Mexico with no problem at all. The car was stopped, but Pepi knew why. The border guard, a rather squatty young man, had spotted Edie and asked her instead of C.C. what they were going to do in Juárez.

Edie ate up his attention, tossing her blond hair and laughing as she told him they were going shopping. He waved them through with flattering reluctance, still eyeing Edie, while C.C. chuckled softly under his breath. Edie did love to make a conquest. She seemed to enjoy letting C.C. know that she could attract other men quite easily.

Watching the woman, Pepi could have sworn that C.C. knew exactly what she was up to. He seemed so cynical about women, as if he knew them inside out and couldn't care less. She happened to glance at him then, and saw that bitter, half-mocking smile on his sensuous mouth.

Before she could look away, he caught her eyes. It was like lightning striking. She had to drag her gaze away.

C.C. drove while Edie leaned over the back seat of his big Ford and talked animatedly to Ben. Pepi shook her head. Even her father wasn't immune to Edie's flirting. He was grinning like a Cheshire cat.

It wasn't a long drive and minutes later, they were in Juárez. And it was only thanks to C.C.'s experience that they found their way around—Juárez was impossible with a map, and worse without one.

The city was deliciously Mexican. They browsed through the endless markets and Edie pleaded until C.C. bought her a ridiculously expensive turquoise necklace. Pepi would have been easier to please. If C.C. had handed her a pebble from the ground, she'd have slept with it under her pillow for the rest of her life. But her tastes were simpler than Edie's—she only wanted C.C.

Down the street was a magnificent cathedral, and near that was a small boutique. Edie exclaimed at the display in the window, and noticed that they honored her charge card.

"I'll only be a few hours," she told C.C., tiptoeing to kiss his lean cheek. "Penelope, want to come along?" she called to Penelope, knowing full well that the younger woman had little interest in fancy clothes and didn't possess a charge card. She'd never gone further afield than the small town she grew up in; Edie knew that, too.

"No, thanks," Pepi said amiably. "I'd rather sight-see."

"Good," her father said. "You can keep me company. C.C. seems to be in another world."

He did, and when Pepi saw where his dark eyes were riveted, she felt her stomach sink. He was mentally re-tracing his steps the night he got drunk, she was sure of it! His eyes went from the bar down the street to a small chapel—the chapel where he'd drunkenly forced Pepi to stand in front of a priest.

"Well, well, a wedding chapel," Ben murmured. He glanced down at Pepi. "For a man who isn't interested in getting married, he does seem to find it fascinating, doesn't he?"

Pepi had a sick feeling when she saw C.C. jam his lean hands into his pockets and start toward the chapel. She moved forward instinctively to try to divert him. And just as she reached him, oblivious to her father's surprised expression, the two Mexicans who'd helped her bundle up C.C. and get him to the truck that night came sauntering out of the wedding chapel. Perhaps they were related to the priest . . .

Don't say anything, don't recognize him, please, she prayed, both her fingers crossed.

They did recognize him, though, and broke into wide grins. *"Felicitaciones,"* they laughed. *"¿Como quiere usted vida conjugal, eh? ¡Y alla esta su esposa! ¿Hóla, señora, coma 'sta?"*

"What?" Ben burst out, overhearing the conversation.

Pepi buried her face in her hands. "What did they say?" she asked through her fingers.

"They're congratulating him on being married!"

Ben didn't say another word. Rapid-fire Spanish exchanges led to an ominous silence, and seconds later, a furious C.C. was towering over her. He took her by both shoulders and shook her, hard, ignoring Ben's dazed presence.

"What the hell do they mean, congratulations on my marriage?" he demanded, his deep voice cutting and sharp. "You lied to me! We were married here that night, weren't we? Weren't we?"

"All right, yes," she whispered. "I didn't know it was legal," she tried to explain, her eyes big, tearful and anguished. "C.C., I didn't know it was legal!"

"You're married?" Ben burst out.

"Not for long," C.C. said, all but throwing Pepi away from him, as if the touch of her burned his hands. "My God, of all the low, contemptible, underhanded ways to get a husband! Get a man drunk and drag him in front of a minister, and then keep it a secret! You knew I'd never marry a plain, plump little schemer like you if I was sober! You're nothing to look at, and you're more man than woman the way you dress and act. It wouldn't surprise me if you told Hale every move to make when you get him in bed!"

"C.C., please," she pleaded, aware of the attention his loud, angry voice was attracting.

He seemed to realize that they were on display. "I'll get Edie. We're leaving, right now," he told Pepi. "The sooner this farce ends in an annulment, the better."

"You got him drunk and married him?" Ben asked, shaken by the revelation.

"He got drunk and threatened to land us in a Mexican jail if I didn't," she said heavily. "I didn't think it was binding anywhere except in Mexico or I'd never have gone through with it. You know what the criminal justice system is like down here, it's as slow as molasses. We could have spent weeks or months in jail before you could have managed to get us out...."

"I know that! What did he mean about you sleeping with Hale?" he demanded.

"I don't sleep with Brandon. I just let C.C. think it... Well, to throw up a smoke screen, I guess. Dad, it's such a mess! I had the best intentions...and on your birthday!" She burst into tears. "I should have said something, but I was scared. I thought I could get a quiet annulment, but the lawyer said he'd have to know...!"

Ben held her while she cried, awkwardly patting her back until a fire-eyed C.C. joined them with Edie in tow.

"What's the matter with Pepi?" Edie asked.

"Don't ask," Ben said heavily. "We have to go."

"Okay," she shrugged, eyeing the younger woman curiously. "Gosh, Pepi, are you sick?"

"If she is, she damn well deserves to be," C.C. said furiously. "Let's go."

Edie didn't dare question him. Pepi cried silently and Ben sat by helplessly while they got out of Juárez into El Paso and on the road to the ranch.

C.C. was out of sorts the whole way back home. He smoked in silence, letting Edie prattle on until she got disgusted with him and turned up the radio. Lost in thoughts of her own, Penelope just leaned back with her eyes closed, oblivious to the worried look on her father's face.

Instead of going to the ranch, C.C. stopped by Edie's apartment, escorted her to the door and left her there without a word. He didn't say another word all the way home. He didn't speed, or drive recklessly. Penelope wondered at his control. Even when he was furious, and she knew he was right now, he never lost that iron control. She wondered if he ever had.

Back at the ranch, C.C. headed for the stables the minute he parked the car, and Pepi felt sorry for any poor soul who was in there undefended. C.C. in a temper was a force to behold. Presumably he was going to work off some steam before he started on her again. She couldn't even blame him for being so angry. She should have told him in the very beginning. It was her own fault.

"Suppose you tell me the whole story?" her father asked while she made coffee in the kitchen.

She did, all about C.C.'s once-a-year bender and the reason for it, about the way she'd sobered him up—or thought she had—and the way she'd trailed him to Juárez and wound up married to him.

"The bottom line," she said, "is that I think he comes from money, despite the work he does here. He might think I deliberately maneuvered him into marriage for mercenary motives."

"C.C. knows you better than that," Ben scoffed.

"He knows the ranch hasn't been paying and that I don't have a job and my future looks pretty insecure," she said. "It isn't, but it looks that way. And I'm reasonably sure he knows that I'm attracted to him."

"Attracted, as in head over heels in love with?" her father mused.

She shook her head. "No, thank God, he doesn't know that." She jammed her hands into her slacks pockets with a heavy sigh. Her eyes were red-rimmed from crying. "It's not the end of the world. We can get an annulment pretty easily, and I'll even get a job and pay for it. Maybe someday he'll forgive me, but right now I guess he'd like to strangle me and I don't blame him. I just hope he doesn't tell Edie. I wouldn't like her to be hurt by it."

"What about you?" Ben asked angrily. "You're hurt by it, and it's his own damned fault. If he'd stayed sober...!"

"Dad, he loved his wife. I guess he's still grieving for her. Remember how you felt when Mom died?" she added.

He got a faraway look in his eyes. He sighed. "Yes, I can understand that. Your mama was my world. We were childhood sweethearts and we lived together for twenty-two years. I could never find anyone to measure up to her, so I never remarried. Maybe he feels like that."

"Maybe he does," she agreed.

He hugged her warmly and let her go. "Try not to brood. It will all pass over. C.C. will blow off steam and come to terms with it, and you'll get it worked out. I hope," he mused on a chuckle. "With times as hard as they are, I need to keep C.C.'s mind on business, with all due respect to you."

"Ever thought of selling shares in the property?" she asked seriously.

"Yes, I have. Or taking on a partner," he added. He glanced at her. "You wouldn't mind if I did that?"

"Of course not. I don't want to lose it, either," she added gently. "You do whatever you have to."

He sighed, looking around the rustic, spacious kitchen. "Then I think I'll do some discreet advertising. God knows, you can't go much longer without a new wardrobe," he added with a mischievous wink.

"Forget about my wardrobe," she returned. "I don't care what I wear. Not anymore," she added, turning back to see about the coffee.

"There's still Hale," he said, trying to comfort her as best he could. Her pain was tangible.

"Yes, there's still Brandon. He's taking me to a cattleman's association dinner next Wednesday night," she said. "He's a nice man, don't you think?"

He studied her quietly. "Sure he is. But you don't love him. Don't settle for crumbs, honey. Go for the whole meal."

She laughed. "Old reprobate," she accused. "You do have a way with words."

"You have a way with food," he countered. "Will you hurry up and get some supper fixed? I'm starving!"

"Okay." She went back to her pots and pans. From the kitchen window, she could see the bunkhouse. C.C. came out suddenly, dressed in, of all things, a suit. He walked toward the house, big and lean and elegant, and she washed the same dish four times while she waited for the step at the kitchen door. C.C. never went to the front. He was too much like family. But right now he was her worst enemy. The suit bothered her. Was he quitting? She felt her heart stop beating momentarily while she brooded. Did he hate her that much . . . ?

He came in without knocking, letting in a chilly burst of wind. Penelope shuddered.

"It's getting colder out there," Ben said to ease the sudden tension.

"Colder than you know," C.C. said. He had a smoking cigarette in his hand. He lifted it to his thin lips, glaring at Pepi. "I'll be away until early next week. I've got some personal business to see to. Including," he added icily, "getting an annulment underway. I want that marriage license, Penelope."

She wiped her hands on her apron, not looking at him. "I'll get it," she said in a subdued tone, and ran for the staircase.

Her hands trembled as she took the piece of paper out of her bureau drawer and looked at it. C. C. Tremayne. The name on the license said Connal Cade Tremayne. Connal. She'd never called him anything but C.C. Until that night in Juárez, she didn't know what the initials stood for. Now she said the name to herself and grieved for the dreams contained in that simple page of words. If only things had been different, and they'd married because he loved her.

She took one long, last look at the license and carried it back downstairs.

C.C. was waiting for her at the foot of the staircase, alone. His black eyes bit into her face, but she wouldn't meet them. She held out the paper in trembling, cold fingers until he took it and then she jerked her hand back before it touched his. She could imagine that he'd welcome her touch about as much as leprosy right now.

"I'm sorry," she said huskily, staring at her boot-clad feet. "It was just—"

"Just an outsize crush that got out of hand," he returned icily. "Well, it backfired, didn't it? You're underhanded and scheming and probably a golddigger to boot."

Hot tears stung her eyes. She didn't answer him. She edged past him and went into the kitchen, barely able to see the floor as she went back to the pots and pans on the stove.

He clenched the license in his lean hand, hating himself, hating her. He was taking the hide off her, and he knew he was being unreasonable, but she'd tricked him into marriage when he was too drunk to know what he was doing. He'd thought better of her. She had no right to land him in this predicament. He'd taken Edie out, he'd... And he was married! What if he'd decided to take Edie to a minister? He'd have been committing unwitting adultery and bigamy all at once!

"She's paying for it," Ben said quietly, joining the younger man in the hall. "Don't make it any worse on her. She didn't do it deliberately, regardless of what you think."

"She should have told me," he returned curtly.

"Yes," Ben agreed. "She should have. But she didn't know how. She didn't think it was legal. And to give her credit, she did call an attorney about a quick, quiet annulment. But she found out she'd need your signature for that."

"Did you know?" C.C. demanded.

Ben shook his head. "Not until today. I thought she was in some kind of trouble, but I had no idea what it was."

C.C. stared at the paper in his hand with angry, troubled eyes. Marriage. A wife. He couldn't forget Marsha, he couldn't forget her determination to go down that river with him. She'd always been headstrong, hell-bent in her own way. He should have insisted, especially since she was sick so often and dizzy. He hadn't known she was pregnant. It had been horrible enough to have to identify her body, but to know that she'd been carrying their first child . . .

He groaned aloud. He'd all but killed her. His wealth had been tied to hers, a joint venture that had paid off in the embryo transplant science. He'd been too sickened by the accident to take up the reins again, leaving his oldest brothers in charge and the younger one to help while he went in search of peace of mind. He'd found it here. He'd enjoyed helping Ben build up a ranch that had been headed for receivership. He'd enjoyed Pepi's bright, undemanding company. And now she'd stabbed him in the back. He had to get away, from her and the memories she'd brought on him again.

"Where are you going?" Ben asked. "Or is that a question I shouldn't ask?"

"What do you mean?"

Ben shrugged. "Pepi said she thought you probably came from money. You blurted a lot out to her that time you were delirious and she nursed you. She thought maybe you'd been punishing yourself for your wife's death and that's why you stayed here." C.C. didn't answer. Ben lifted an eyebrow. "Whatever the reason, you're welcome here if you want to come back. I'm grateful for all you've done for me."

C.C. felt doors closing. Ben was talking as if he wasn't coming back. He glanced toward the kitchen, but Pepi was not visible there. He felt a sudden shock of panic at the thought of not seeing her again. God, what was wrong with him?

He folded the marriage license. "I don't know what I'm going to do. I might go home and see my people. I need to make an appointment with a lawyer about this," he added, fingering the paper. Odd how it seemed more like a treasure than an unwanted legal tie.

"Well, if you decide not to come back, I won't blame you," Ben said wearily. "Not much hope for this place, and we both know it. You've got us in the black, but cattle prices are down and I had to go in the hole for more equipment. I'm getting too old to manage, anyway."

That didn't sound like Ben. C.C. scowled. "My God, you're barely fifty-five!"

"Wait until *you're* fifty-five and say that," Ben chuckled. He held out a hand and C.C. shook it. "Thanks for giving me a shot at keeping the place. But you've got your own life to live." His eyes narrowed. "Maybe it's time you faced your ghosts, son. I had to do that, when I finally came to grips with my drinking problem and the fact that it cost me Pepi's mother. I survived. So will you."

"Marsha was pregnant," C.C. said curtly.

Ben nodded. "That's the worst of it for you, I imagine. You're a young man, C.C. Comparatively young, anyway. You can have other children."

"I don't want children. I don't want a wife," he said angrily, shaking the marriage license. "Least of all one I didn't choose!"

In the kitchen, Pepi heard his words, and tears rolled silently down her cheeks. She remembered what he'd said to her in Juárez, about her being plump and plain. It certainly wiped out all the former compliments he'd given her, about being womanly looking. Now he just thought she was fat. She wished she could crawl in a hole and die.

Out in the hall, Ben could imagine Pepi's pain. He herded C.C. toward the front door instead of the back one, to spare Pepi any more anguish.

"Take a few days," Ben suggested. "You've had two hard weeks of roundup and you haven't had a real vacation in over three years. Some time off is just the thing."

C.C. relaxed a little. "I guess I do need it." He stared at the folded license and involuntarily, his eyes went back down the hall. He'd been harder on Pepi than he probably should have been. He frowned, remembering what he'd said to her. She was little more than a child in some ways. He was beginning to wonder if her so-called experience wasn't just a figment of her imagination. The way she'd reacted to him in the kitchen that morning hadn't been indicative of sophistication. Could she have lied about that, too?

His jaw clenched. He'd never be able to trust her again. If she'd lie to him once, she'd do it twice. God, why had she done this to him?

"Go on," Ben said gently, wary of new explosions. "I can handle things until you get back. Or until I have to look for a new foreman. I won't pressure you."

He frowned, thinking about something Ben had said. "You said she knew I had money."

Ben grimaced. "Yes, I did. And she was sure you'd think the marriage was because of it." He shook his head. "You're doing your damnedest to paint her evil through and through, aren't you, son?"

C.C. blinked. Was he? He moved restlessly. "I'll be in touch. Sorry to leave you in the lurch like this. God knows, it's not your fault."

"It's not Pepi's, either," Ben said enigmatically. "When you want to know the whole story, you might ask her side of it. But cool down first. And have a safe trip."

C.C. started to say something, but he closed his mouth. "Take care of yourself. Happy Birthday," he added, withdrawing a small package from his breast pocket. "I wish it could have been a happier one."

"I'm getting a whole coconut cake," Ben reminded him. He grinned. "Nothing makes me happier than not having to share it."

C.C. chuckled softly. "Okay. See you."

"Yes. I hope so," Ben added under his breath when the younger man had gone. He opened the package. It was a tie tack with a gold maverick head. He grinned. Leave it to C.C. to pick something he really liked.

He went back into the kitchen, hesitant about approaching Pepi. But she was calm enough, dishing up supper.

"Ready to eat?" she asked pleasantly. Only the faint redness of her eyes attested to her earlier misery.

"Sure. You all right?" Ben asked.

She nodded. "Right as rain. There's just one thing. I don't want to talk about it. Ever. Okay?"

He agreed. And she was her old self, on the surface at least. What Ben couldn't see was the agony under her calm expression, the pain in her heart. She was sure she didn't love C.C. now. A man who could be that cruel didn't deserve to be loved, and it was his fault anyway. He was the one who'd forced her to get married. But he made it sound like she'd trapped him! Well, they'd see about that when he came back again. He'd never have to worry about having her heart at his feet ever again!

She served her father his favorite foods for supper and gave him his present—a new pipe and a special lighter for it—with a huge slice of coconut cake. She pretended to be happy, and hoped he wouldn't see the truth. She didn't want to spoil the rest of his birthday.

"There's just one thing you might think about," he said before she went up to bed later. "A man who's caught against his will isn't going to give in without a fight."

"I didn't catch—!" she fumed.

"You aren't listening. I mean a man who's fighting his own feelings, Pepi. I think he's got a case on you, and he doesn't want to face it. He won't take it lying down. He'll give you hell until he accepts it."

She knew better than to let herself dream again. She couldn't take another disappointment in love. "I don't want him anymore," she said bluntly. "I should have married Brandon in the first place. At least he doesn't yell at me and accuse me of things I didn't do. He's fun to be with and even if I don't love him, I like him. I sure as hell don't like C. C. Tremayne!"

"Don't marry one man trying to forget another one," Ben cautioned. "It'll only hurt Brandon and yourself."

She sighed. "I guess so. But I might learn to love him. I'm going to do my best to love him. I hope C. C. Tremayne never comes back!"

"God forbid. If that happens, the ranch will go under," Ben chuckled.

She threw up her hands and climbed the staircase.

But she didn't sleep. She wondered if she ever would again. She felt sick all over, hearing C.C.'s angry words every time she closed her eyes. Eventually she gave up even trying to go to sleep. She got up and cleaned the kitchen until dawn, an exercise that proved adequate to take her mind off C.C.—for two minute stretches, at least.

By the time Ben had finished his breakfast, she was dressed for church. He didn't say a word. He went and put on his suit and they drove to the little Methodist church five miles down the road.

When they got home, with Pepi still brooding and withdrawn, Brandon Hale's car was parked at the front steps. She got out of her father's car and ran to Brandon as fast as her legs would carry her.

Ben, watching, frowned. Trouble was sitting on the horizon, and he wondered where this new complication was going to land them all.

Chapter Six

Brandon gaped at Pepi when she told him what was going on. They'd just finished a sparse lunch and her father was bringing the coffee tray into the living room where they were sitting.

"You're married?" Brandon groaned.

"Not really," she said quickly. She fingered her skirt while she gave him the details. "So, you see, it's just legal on paper, and only until I can get it annulled."

"C.C. knows, I guess?" Brandon persisted.

"Boy, does he know!" Ben Mathews muttered. He brought in a tray with three cups of black coffee on it. "If any of you want cream, you can go get it," he added as he put it down on the coffee table in the early American decor of the living room.

"Well, what did he say?" the younger man asked.

"You couldn't repeat it in mixed company." Ben sighed.

"He was furious," Pepi volunteered. She stared at her skirt. "I guess I can't blame him. He doesn't know the whole story, and I was too upset to try to make him listen. It doesn't matter anyway," she said miserably. "He said he sure didn't want to be married to somebody like me."

"He was in shock," Ben said stubbornly, staring at her averted face. "A man has to have time to adjust to news like that."

"How long will an annulment take?" Brandon asked.

"I'll find out in the morning. I'm going to see our attorney," Pepi told him. "Maybe it won't take long. Heaven knows, C.C. will do his best to rush it through. I hope I don't have to have the marriage license," she added, frowning. "C.C. took it with him."

"Where'd he go?" Brandon asked.

"¿Quien sabe?" Ben shrugged.

"At least it's not a real marriage," Brandon said gently, patting Pepi's soft hand in her lap. "You scared the life out of me."

"Well, it's definitely not real, so you can relax," Pepi said. "Drink your coffee, Brandon. Then we can go riding. I need to get out of the house."

"Good idea," Ben seconded. "And I can start on the books."

"It's Sunday!" she protested.

"I know that. I'll eat my cake while I work on them. That will make it all right. Besides," he chuckled wickedly, "we went to church first."

She threw up her hands and went to change into jeans and a T-shirt.

Brandon stayed until late, and Pepi was glad of his company. She hardly slept that night, and early the next morning she went to see the family attorney.

Mr. Hardy was sixty and very abrupt, but under his bespectacled, dignified manner, he was the best friend that the Mathews family had ever had.

"Don't have the license, hmm?" he murmured when Pepi had told him the whole story. "No matter. I'll go ahead and draw up the papers for the annulment. Have C.C. come in and sign them Friday. Meanwhile, don't worry about it. Just one of those things. But if I were him, I'd keep away from liquor from now on," he added dryly.

She smiled. "I'll try to make sure he does that," she replied gently.

There, she told herself later, it was done. The wheels were in motion. In no time, she'd be plain old Penelope Mathews again, not Penelope Tremayne. The thought depressed her. She'd wanted so badly to keep the name, to have the marriage real and wanted. But C.C. had made no secret of his feelings on the matter, or of his patent disgust with the idea of Pepi as a wife. She wondered if she was ever going to be able to forget the wounding things he'd said to her.

On an impulse, she stopped by the local department of labor office to see what kinds of jobs were going for women with minimum typing skills. Fate was kind. There was a receptionist's job open with a local insurance agency. She went over to inquire about it, and was hired. She was to start on the following Monday, a week away— on the condition that their valued receptionist, who'd just had a baby, stuck to her decision not to return. They couldn't refuse her if she wanted her job back, and they promised to call Pepi if she wasn't needed.

Well, if that didn't work out, she'd find something else, she promised herself. There was just no way she could stay on the ranch now that this fiasco had occurred. Every time she saw C.C., it would rip her heart open. And if he made fun of her, or taunted her about the almost-marriage, it would be unbearable. Probably he still hated her. That might make it easier. Ben needed him, so she couldn't demand that he be fired. She'd just have to find a graceful way out of the dilemma for all of them. Despite the hurt, she loved C.C. more than her own life. She could leave the ranch and find a room in El Paso, and a job. That way her father could have his very necessary foreman and she could have peace of mind. Besides, Brandon lived in El Paso. He'd look out for her. She might even marry him. He was kind and he cared about her. Surely that was better than living alone.

By Wednesday afternoon, C.C. still hadn't come back. Wednesday night, Brandon took Pepi to a cattleman's association meeting with him. It was a dinner meeting, and Pepi enjoyed not only the meal but the discussion about range improvement methods that followed it.

She'd worn a new mustard-colored rayon skirt with her knee-high lace-up Apache moccasins and a Western-cut patterned blouse. Her reddish-brown hair was around her shoulders for a change, and she'd put on enough make-up to embellish her face. She looked pretty, and Brandon's interest was echoed by several single men present.

Her drooping spirits got quite a lift. She smiled and talked and laughed, and by the time they left the meeting, she was relaxed and happy.

That mood lasted until they got to the front porch and Brandon bent to kiss her good-night. Before he reached her lips, a coldly unapproachable C.C. sauntered into the light from the darkened corner where he'd been sitting.

"Oh, hello, C.C.," Brandon said hesitantly. He raked a hand through his red hair, glancing worriedly at Pepi's suddenly white face. "I'll call you in the morning, Pepi. Good night!"

He darted off the porch. Pepi watched him go so that she wouldn't have to look at C.C. One glimpse told her that he was wearing a charcoal-gray suit with a pearly Stetson, and that he looked dangerous. Smoke from the cigarette in his lean fingers drifted past her nose as Brandon waved and drove out of the yard.

"Where have you been?" he asked, his deep voice accusing.

"I've been to a cattleman's association meeting, C.C.," she replied, moving unobtrusively away from the threat of his powerful body. She turned and went into the house, leaving C.C. to close the door behind them.

"No word of welcome?" he asked sarcastically.

She didn't look at him. She couldn't bear to see the expression in his eyes. She started toward the staircase, but he reached out to catch her arm.

Her reaction caught him off guard. She jerked her arm away from his lean hand and backed against the staircase, her wide, dark eyes accusing and frightened.

His thin lips parted on a sharp breath. "My God, you're not afraid of me?" he asked, scowling.

"I'm tired," she said, averting her face. "I just want to go to bed. Mr. Hardy says you can come in and sign the annulment papers Friday," she added. "I started proceedings and I'll pay for them. You won't have to be out a penny. Is Dad in his study?"

He frowned as he lifted the cigarette to his lips. "He's over at the bunkhouse, talking to Jed. I don't want you seeing Hale while you're legally married to me."

She hesitated, but it wasn't really much to ask. And she was too tired to argue with him. "All right, C.C.," she replied dully. "Maybe the annulment won't take too long."

His eyes narrowed to angry slits. "In a hurry to put Hale's ring on your finger?" he asked.

"I don't want to fight with you," she said quietly, meeting his gaze with an effort. It disturbed her, the way he was looking at her. It made her heart race, her knees tremble under her. "I've got a job," she told him. "I start Monday. Then I'll look for a room or something in El Paso. You won't . . . You won't have to worry about running into me all the time around here."

"Pepi!" he said huskily.

She whirled. "Good night, C.C.!"

She ran all the way upstairs and into her room, closing the door with hands that trembled, with tears running down her pale cheeks. So he was back. Back, and spoiling for trouble. That didn't bode well for the future.

She got into her gown, washed her face, and climbed into bed with a long sigh. She was reaching for the bedside light when her door suddenly opened and C.C. came in, closing it behind him.

Pepi froze with her hand out, all too aware of the way the almost transparent green gown she was wearing outlined her body, left the upper curve of her breasts bare. With her hair around her pale shoulders, she looked very soft and feminine, and C.C. was getting an eyeful.

"What do you want?" she asked uneasily.

"To talk," he replied. He pulled up a chair beside the bed and dropped into it. There were new lines in his face, and he looked as tired as she felt. He'd discarded his suit coat and tie and rolled up the sleeves of his exquisite cotton shirt, its neck unbuttoned to his collarbone. Dark curly hair peeked out between the loose buttons and Pepi had to force her eyes back up to his face. She didn't like being reminded of his vibrant masculinity. She wasn't his type, and he didn't want her. She had to remember that.

"About the annulment?" she asked hesitantly. She sat up against her pillow, demurely pulling the sheet over her breasts, an action that C.C.'s faintly amused eyes didn't miss.

He watched her hungrily. The days he'd been away, a lot of things had been settled in his mind. He'd brooded about his own situation until he'd given some thought to Pepi's. That was when he'd realized how much he owed her. She'd been the best friend he had, ever since he'd come to the ranch. But he'd repaid her loyalty by hurting her, making her feel unwanted. Now he had to put things right, if he could. Perhaps telling her the truth about his past might be a good first step. If she understood him, she might be able to forgive the things he'd said to her before he left.

"No," he said after a minute. "I don't want to talk about the annulment right now. I want to tell you about me." He leaned back in the chair and crossed one long leg over the other. "I was born in Jacobsville, down near Victoria," he began, watching her while he lit a cigarette and fished for an ashtray on the dresser. He grimaced as he emptied jewelry out of it and put it in his lap. "I have three brothers, two older, one younger than I am. We're in the cattle business, too, except that we deal in purebred cattle—Santa Gertrudis. Our land came from one of the early Spanish land grants, and we've always had money."

She watched him, astonished at the revelation.

"I got married years ago. I was getting older, I was lonely," he shrugged. "I wanted her. She was my age, and a wild woman from the word go. We both liked dangerous sports, like shooting the white water.'' His fingers clenched on the cigarette, and there was suddenly a faraway, tormented look in his dark eyes. ''She went everywhere with me. But that weekend, I wanted to get away. She had this tendency to smother me; had to be with me every minute, night and day. After the first few weeks we were married, it got so I couldn't stand and talk to one of my brothers without having her in my pocket. She was insanely jealous, but I hadn't realized that until it was too late. Well, I signed up for a rafting trip down the Colorado and went without her. But when I got to the river with the rest of the group, she was there waiting. We argued. It didn't do any good. She was hell-bent on going.'' He took a draw from the cigarette. ''The raft capsized on a bad stretch and she went under. We searched for the better part of an hour, but by the time we found her, it was too late.'' He looked straight at Pepi, his eyes cold. ''She was three months pregnant.''

''I'm sorry,'' she said quietly. ''That must have been the worst of it, for you.''

He was surprised at her perceptiveness, although God knew why he should have been. Pepi always managed to see things that other people missed. ''Yes, that was the worst of it,'' he confessed. ''I was never able to find out if she knew about her condition, or if she didn't care. She was a free spirit. She wasn't really suited to marriage. If she'd stayed single, she'd probably still be alive.''

''I'm a fatalist,'' Pepi said, her voice gentle. ''I think God chooses when we die, and the circumstances.''

''Perhaps you're right. But it's taken me three years to come to grips with it. I inherited her estate, and she was as wealthy as I was. That was one reason I came here, started over again from scratch with your father. I wanted to get away from money and see what I could do by the sweat of my own brow. I inherited most of what I had. It's been fun, making my own way."

"It's been a lifesaving experience for us," Pepi said. "We owe you a lot. And you were a mystery to us, but you always seemed to fit in very well."

"Except for one day a year," he mused sadly. "Every year on the day it happened, I go a little crazy. I didn't know how much I wanted a child until it was too late."

She searched for the right words to comfort him. "C.C., you're still young enough to marry again and have children," she said hesitantly.

His eyes narrowed. "But I am married, Pepi. To you."

She felt her cheeks stinging with heat. She averted her wounded eyes to the coverlet. "Not for long. Mr. Hardy said an annulment would be no problem at all."

"I'd like to know what happened that night," he said after a minute.

"Not a lot. You were stinking drunk in a bar in Juárez. I went in to get you out, you made a lot of insulting remarks, and then you said since I seemed to be forever nursemaiding you, I might as well marry you. In fact, you threatened to land us in jail if I didn't."

His eyebrows arched. "I did?"

"You did," she muttered. "I wasn't sure what to think. You were pretty loud and you sounded serious to me. Mexican jails are easy to get into and hard to get out of. I had visions of us languishing down there for months while Dad went nuts trying to get us out."

"My God! Why didn't you tell me that?"

"You didn't want to listen," she replied doggedly. "You were too busy telling me what an underhanded little golddigger I was!"

He sighed angrily. "I know plenty about golddiggers," he said defensively. "Until I married, I fielded them like baseballs."

"You never had to field me!" Pepi returned. She glared at him from the depths of her feather pillow. "I looked after you when you needed it and I liked to think we were friends, but that's all it was," she lied, salvaging what she could of her pride. "I never wanted to marry you!"

His dark eyes narrowed as he turned that statement over in his mind and examined it. He didn't believe her. She'd been vulnerable to him before he'd hurt her pride so badly. If any feeling was still there, he might be able to reach it if he was careful, and slow.

"I remember telling you once that I had nothing left of love in me," he said. "It felt like that, for a long time. I got numb, I think, because of the guilt. I wouldn't let myself feel."

She lowered her eyes to his chest. "Yes, I can understand that," she said gently. "But I was never any threat to you, C.C."

"Weren't you?" he mused, smiling faintly. "You were the most caring little thing I'd ever met. You mothered me. Funny, how much I enjoyed that after a while. Apple pie when I was broody, hot stew when I was cold, unexpected things like puff pastries in my saddlebags when I went out to roundup. Oh, you got under my skin, Pepi, right from the beginning. The miracle is that I didn't realize how far."

"You don't have to baby me," she muttered, glaring at him. "What you said when you found out we were married was the truth. It was honest. I always knew you wouldn't want a fat frump like me...."

"Pepi!"

"Well, I am one," she said doggedly, her fingers clenching in the cover. "Ugly and overweight and country to the bone. Dad used to say that you were sophisticated enough for a debutante, and he was right. Edie's just your style."

He leaned back in his chair. "Edie doesn't want a house in the country and two or three kids," he said quietly.

So that was it. He couldn't have Edie, so he might be willing to settle for second-best—for Pepi. She lowered her eyes. She'd wanted him for so long that she was almost ready to take him on any terms, even on the rebound. But she couldn't forget the things he'd said about her, and to her.

"You might be able to change her mind," she said.

He scowled, watching her. "I don't want to change it," he said surprisingly. "Pepi, we're married."

She colored. "That isn't a hurdle. I told you, I've already seen Mr. Hardy. All you have to do is sign the papers on Friday and he'll get the annulment underway."

He felt that statement to his bones. He shifted in the chair, his gaze on her flushed face. "You haven't considered the options. Your father is still just barely operating in the black. I could put the ranch back on its feet for good. You might find a few things that you wanted, too. After all, I'm rich."

"I don't care about your money," she returned, her pale brown eyes accusing. "I like having food in the house and a roof over my head, but I couldn't care less about how much money I've got, and you know it!"

His breath sighed out roughly. "Is it Hale?" he demanded. "Is he why you're in such a rush to get an annulment?"

Her eyes dilated. "*You're* the one who was demanding a speedy end to the marriage!"

"Yes, well, I've had second thoughts." He uncrossed his legs and sprawled, one hand loosely grasping the almost-finished cigarette as he stared at her. "If I'm already married, I won't have to fend off potential brides, will I?" he added.

She sat up straight in bed. "Now, you listen here, C.C., I'm not going to become a human sacrifice to save you from the altar! Marrying you sure wasn't my idea!"

"You could have called my bluff," he reminded her, his dark eyes faintly twinkling. "Why didn't you?"

"I told you! Because I didn't want to spend the rest of my life in a Mexican jail!"

"If I was drunk enough to pass out, I was too drunk to cause much trouble," he continued. "Besides, I didn't have a gun."

She drew up her knees angrily and clasped her arms around them. "You've got all the answers, haven't you?"

"Not quite all," he said. "But I'm getting there." He took his time, stabbing out his cigarette in the ashtray. "You said once that you and Hale were lovers. Are you?" he asked, lifting his eyes back to hers.

She gave him a wary look, hoping he hadn't seen through the lie. If he thought she and Brandon were close, it might keep him at bay until she could decide how to cope with this newest complication. "That's none of your business."

"The hell it's not. You're mine."

Electricity danced through her veins, but she didn't let him see the reaction in her eyes. "No, I am not. You're only married to me because of an accident. That means Brandon is none of your concern."

He got up with deceptive laziness and put the ashtray back on the side table. "I'm making him my business." He paused at her bedside, narrow eyes assessing, threatening. "You aren't sleeping with him again," he said shortly. "And no more dates, either. From now on, you'll stay at home where you belong."

Her eyes opened wide. "Who do you think you are?" she demanded.

"Your husband," he said, "*Mrs.* Tremayne."

"Don't call me that," she grumbled. "It's not my name."

"Oh, yes, it is. And you can forget that annulment. I won't sign the papers."

"But, you have to!" she said helplessly.

"Really? Why?" he asked, and looked interested.

"Because it's the only way to get rid of me!"

He pursed his lips and let his eyes slide over her. "Do I want to do that? After all, you've been looking out for me for the past three years, through thick and thin. You're a treasure, Pepi. I don't intend giving you up to the redheaded vet. You can tell him I said so."

"I don't want to be married to you," she yelled.

He lifted his eyebrows. "How do you know that? I haven't made love to you yet."

She went scarlet. Her fingers grasped the covers in a death-grip and she stiffened when he took a step closer to the bed, her eyes as wide as saucers in her flushed face.

He shook his head and made a clicking sound with his tongue. "My God, if you keep up this attitude, it's going to be damned hard for us to have children together."

"I won't have children!" she whispered.

"Well, not like that," he murmured, grinning. "You *do* know how women get them?"

"Sure," she said hesitantly. "From the hospital."

"That comes later," he reminded her. He smiled. "Afterward."

That slow, meaningful smile made her nervous. "I don't want to sleep with you," she told him.

"We won't sleep," he promised.

"Will you get out of here!"

Before he could reply, the bedroom door opened suddenly and her father glanced from one of them to the other, scowling. "For God's sake, what's all the yelling about?"

"I've been explaining the facts of life to Pepi." C.C. shrugged. "She thinks babies came from the hospital. Did you tell her that?"

Ben looked flustered. "Well, not exactly... Look here, what are you doing in her bedroom?"

"We're married," C.C. reminded him. He produced an envelope. "The marriage license is in here."

"But you don't want to be married to her," Ben returned. "You said so. You went off to get an annulment."

"I changed my mind. She's a good cook, she's nice looking, and she doesn't have any bad habits. I could do worse."

"I could do better!" Pepi shouted, red-faced. "You get out of here, Connal Tremayne! I'm getting that annulment, and you can go to hell!"

C.C. exchanged an amused glance with Ben. "I suppose you taught her to swear, too?" he asked the older man. "For shame!"

"She taught me," Ben said defensively. "And I don't think she wants to say married to you, C.C."

"Sure she does!" he replied. "It's just going to take a little time to convince her of it. Meanwhile—" he threw an arm across the older man's shoulder "—I want to talk to you about some improvements I have in mind for the house and the ranch."

"Don't you listen!" Pepi raged. "He's trying to buy us!"

"I am not!" C.C. said indignantly. "I'm trying to overcome your objections. Your father wouldn't mind a partner, I'll bet. Especially when it's his own brand-new son-in-law. Right, Dad?" he added, smiling with crocodile intensity at the older man.

"Right, son!" Ben agreed, grinning back. "I hadn't thought about that," he mused to himself. "I'll finally have a son of my own!"

"Are you both forgetting something?" Pepi asked haughtily.

"I don't think so," C.C. replied.

"I'm not staying married to you!" she told him. "I'm getting an annulment."

"Don't worry, Dad," C.C. told Ben encouragingly. "She has to have my cooperation for that, and I'll never agree. Imagine a woman hard-hearted enough to try to get rid of a man even before the honeymoon!"

"Say, that's right, you haven't had a honeymoon," Ben agreed.

"C.C. can go on the honeymoon by himself," Pepi said. "I hear it's nice in Canada this time of year. Don't they have grizzly bears up there...?"

"We don't have time for a honeymoon just now," C.C. replied easily. "We've got too much work to do fixing up the ranch. First, I thought we'd get a contractor over here and let him look at the house. I'm inviting my brothers up from Jacobsville to talk to us about getting one or two Santa Gertrudis seed bulls..."

"Stop!" Pepi held up her hand. "I won't agree to this!"

"What do you have to do with it?" C.C. asked innocently. "Your father and I are going to be partners."

"Dad, you can't let him do this," she pleaded with her parent.

Ben lifted his eyebrows. "Why not?" he asked.

"She's only frustrated," C.C. said, leading the older man out the door. "A little loving will put her on the right track in no time."

"You try it and I'll crack your head with a tire iron!" she raged.

C.C. grinned at her from the doorway. "I do like a woman with spirit," he murmured.

"Will you please leave?" she said, admitting defeat. "I want to go to sleep."

"You might as well. Maybe it will improve your mood," he said as he closed the door.

"Improve my mood," she muttered, glaring at the closed door. "First he insults me, then he storms off in a snit demanding an annulment and now he wants to go partners with Dad. I will never understand men as long as I live!"

She put her head under the pillow. But despite her best attempts, it was early morning before she finally got to sleep.

Chapter Seven

It wasn't at all unusual for C.C. to have breakfast with Pepi and her father, but in recent months he'd kept very much to himself. Even so, Pepi wasn't surprised to find him sitting in the dining room with her father when she came down to breakfast. She was surprised to find food on the table, waiting for her, right down to a fresh pot of coffee.

"Shocked, are we?" C.C. murmured dryly, his dark eyes sliding possessively down her body, clad in jeans and boots and a white blouse with a yellow knit pullover sweater. "Think men are helpless, do we?"

She glanced around, looking to see how many people he was talking to.

"Cute," he chuckled. "Sit down and eat, before it gets cold."

She took the chair across from him, next to her father. Her gaze went restlessly from C.C. in working clothes—denim and chambray—to her father in a suit.

"Are you planning to be buried before the end of the day, or are you going somewhere?" she asked Ben.

"I'm going to the bank to pay off the note on the place," he said hesitantly.

"With what?" she cried.

"We can talk about it later," C.C. interrupted. "Eat your eggs."

"With what?" she persisted, glaring at her father. He looked guilty. Her eyes went to a smug C.C., leaning back like a conqueror with his shirt straining over a muscular chest and broad shoulders while he watched her. "You did it. You gave him the money to pay off the note, didn't you?" she demanded.

"He's my father-in-law," C.C. said easily. "Not to mention my partner. We're having the papers drawn up today. Your father is seeing about it while he's in town."

"You aren't going with him?" she asked warily.

He shrugged. "We've got a new shipment of cattle coming in. Somebody has to be here to sign for them and oversee the unloading."

"New cattle?" She knew her eyes were bulging. "What new cattle?"

"Some heifers to add to our replacement heifers, that's all," C.C. assured her. He grinned. "But we're going to have two purebred Santa Gertrudis bulls. My brothers are coming up tomorrow."

"There are more like you?" she wondered aloud, recalling his vague reference to them the night before.

"Three," he reminded her.

"God help us all. Are they married?"

His dark eyes narrowed. "One of them is. The youngest. The older two are still single, and don't get any ideas. You've already got a husband."

"Only until I can get your signature on a document," she replied sweetly.

"And hell will freeze over, first," he returned.

"Can't we save the arguing for later?" Ben moaned. "I want to enjoy my breakfast."

"He's got a point. Have some salsa."

She gave up. She spooned the brilliant red salsa over her eggs and savored the spicy flavor they gave the perfectly cooked scrambled eggs. The bacon was neatly done, too, and the biscuits were even better than her own.

She frowned at C.C. She knew that he, like most of the men, could whip up a meal when he had to. But this was beyond the scope of most men who weren't professional chefs. "You cooked all this?"

"Did I say that?" C.C. asked innocently.

"Well, no..."

"Consuelo did it," Ben told her. "We thought you might like a late morning, what with all the excitement last night."

"Excitement," she muttered. "First he wants an annulment and now he doesn't want one."

"Let's just say that I came to my senses in time," C.C. said lazily, smiling at her over a forkful of eggs. His gaze went to her full lips and lingered there, before it slid back up to catch and hold hers. "I know a good thing when I see it."

Her heart went crazy. It wasn't fair, to do this to her. "Why do you need me to ward off prospective brides?" she managed in a husky tone.

"Because I'm going to start a small branch of the family business over here," he replied. "Most people in southeastern Texas know the Tremayne properties. Pretty soon they'll know them in El Peso, and I'll be on the endangered species list. That's where you come in. If I have too many money-hungry women after me, all I have to do is produce my sweet little wife to ward them off.''

''I'm not sweet and I'm not little.'' She put down her fork. ''I'm plain and fat, you said so.''

His jaw clenched. ''I said a lot of things I regret,'' he replied. ''I hope you're not going to spend the next twenty years throwing them in my face every time you get hot under the collar.''

She stared at him until she had to drop her eyes to her plate in self-defense. That level, unblinking stare of his had backed down grown men in a temper. She shifted under it. ''You said you didn't want to get married.''

''I didn't. But it's something of a *fait accompli*, now, isn't it?''

''A what?'' she frowned.

He lifted an eyebrow. ''It's French. It means an accomplished fact. You don't speak French, I gather. I do. I'll teach you. It's a sexy language. So is Spanish.''

She cleared her throat and sipped coffee. ''I don't have a facility for languages.''

''A few words won't hurt you. Especially,'' he added softly, ''the right kind of words.''

She knew what he was insinuating. Her gaze went helplessly to his face and slid to his thin, firm mouth. She'd always wondered how it would feel on hers, but in three years he'd never really kissed her, unless she counted a peck on the lips under the mistletoe that time, and that was as impersonal as a smile. She'd dreamed and dreamed about his arms around her, the pleasure of having him kiss her in a fever of passion. Of course, she wasn't the kind of woman who inspired passion in men. Edie was.

Edie. She thought about the other woman and felt uneasy all over again. She had a pretty good idea what C.C.

had seen in Edie and she wondered if he planned to continue that relationship. The marriage was by no means a real one. He could claim that Pepi had no right to tell him what he could and couldn't do, and he'd be right. They were only married in name.

She put down her fork, her appetite gone. If only he loved her. If only he'd married her voluntarily, and not because of a drunken rampage.

"What's the matter now?" her father muttered, watching her expression change. "You look like the end of the world."

"I couldn't sleep," she said defensively.

"Dreaming about me." C.C. grinned.

She glared at him. "I was not!"

"That's right, Pepi, fight it. But I'll win," he added quietly, getting to his feet to stare down at her. "And you know it."

She didn't understand his new attitude, or that look in his dark eyes, either. She looked up at him helplessly.

"All at sea, aren't you, little one?" he murmured. "Well, it's going to take some time, but you'll get the idea eventually. See you later, Ben." He tossed down the rest of his coffee, retrieved his Stetson from the counter and slanted it across his eyes. "Why don't you come down to the loading dock and watch us move the cattle in?" he asked Pepi.

It was the first such invitation he'd ever extended to her, almost as if he'd welcome her company. She didn't know how to respond to it, so she hesitated.

"Suit yourself," he said on a heavy sigh. "If you change your mind, you know where I'll be."

He went out the door and Pepi exchanged a puzzled glance with her father.

"What's going on?" she asked him.

"Damned if I know, except that he's sure done a hard about-face," Ben replied. "I can't say I'm sorry, in one respect. This land has been in our family since just after the Civil War. I'd hate like hell to lose it, because of my own financial incompetence."

Pepi knew how much the ranch meant to her father, and she felt a twinge of guilt for putting up a fight when C.C. was the answer to all his problems. But he was the root of all hers.

"How do you really feel about this?" Ben asked quietly.

She fingered her coffee cup. "I think he's just making the most of a bad situation," she said. "Or maybe he feels that getting an annulment would be a reflection on his masculinity." She shrugged. "Maybe it's even what he said, to keep prospective brides off his back when his monied background gets around. But how I feel about it is uneasy. He's too smooth about it for a man who was ranting and raving like a madman when he found out what happened in Juárez."

"He was away for several days," Ben said thoughtfully. "Maybe he came to grips with it then."

She remembered what C.C. had told her about his wife, and she wasn't sure about that. He'd mentioned wanting a family, that Edie didn't. He could just be thinking about how easily Pepi could be cast in the mold he wanted—housewife and mother and cook, somebody in the background of his life, somebody he could walk away from without his emotions being involved if the marriage dissolved for any reason. She knew he didn't love her. He'd made that all too obvious already. He might want her. She wasn't even sure about that, because he only let things show on his face that he wanted people to see. He might be playing a game. He might be getting even.

"You're doing it again," Ben observed. "Brooding," he added when she frowned with curiosity. "Stop brooding. Live one day at a time and see what happens."

She wanted to argue, but there was really no reason to. "Okay," she said easily. "I've got a job," she said.

"A what?"

"A job. Well, I've almost got a job," she amended. "There's one going in El Paso, if the receptionist who just had a baby doesn't come back." She told him about it, puzzled by his worried look. "What's wrong with my having a job?" she demanded.

"You've got enough to do around here," he muttered. "I'll have to give up my apple pies and cakes if you go to work. Who'll take care of me?"

Her eyebrows arched. "But, Dad, I can't stay at home forever!"

"Could if you stayed married to my new son-in-law," he said curtly. "No reason why you shouldn't. He's a great catch. Rich, good-looking, smart..."

"...hardheaded, autocratic, unreasonable..." she amended.

"...and best of all, he likes kids," he concluded firmly. "I like kids. Would have had more than just you if we could have, you know. Nothing in the world I'd enjoy more than a houseful of grandkids."

"Great. When I get free from C.C. and marry Brandon, we'll make sure you have lots. All redheaded," she said with a smug grin.

"I don't want redheaded grandkids!" he raged.

"Too bad," she sighed, finishing her breakfast. "Because I'm not going to spend the rest of *my* life helping C.C. ward off women."

"Hasn't it occurred to you that he might have other reasons for wanting you to stay with him?" her father asked after a minute. "More personal reasons than he's given?"

She searched his face. "You mean because of his wife, and the baby?" she asked.

He nodded. "Hard for him, losing her like that, and her pregnant at the time. I can see why he's haunted. I know all about guilt, sweetheart, I felt it for years because I was drinking the night of the wreck that killed your mother. I learned finally that you can't live in the past. You have to shoulder your mistakes and regrets and go on. He's learning that. Maybe he's ready to start over, too."

"Maybe he is, but it's not enough, Dad," she said wearily. "I can't be just a healing balm in his life, you know? I have to be loved, wanted, needed."

"He needs you, all right, we've all seen that over the years," Ben reminded her.

"Sure. Good old Pepi, keeping him out of trouble, making sure he wears his raincoat, watching over his meals...but that isn't what he needs, Dad. He needs a woman he can love. Edie would be a better choice than I am, at least they've got a relationship of sorts. C.C. and I—well, he's never even kissed me," she muttered with a faint flush.

"You might ask him to, then," Ben said with a twinkle in his eyes. "Just to sample the goods, so to speak."

She went redder and lowered her brown eyes to her plate. "I don't want to kiss him, I don't know where he's been."

"You won't know what you're missing until you try," he said. "After all, you've lived like a saint for the past few years, despite the best efforts of the redheaded vet."

"You didn't tell C.C. that!" she exclaimed.

"He figured it for himself," he said easily. "C.C.'s been around. Even a blind man could tell that you haven't. You blush too much."

"I'll dot my face with rice powder and wear a mask over my eyes from now on, that's for sure!" she grumbled. "Men!"

"Now, now. We only want what's best for you."

"And the fact that he can get the ranch out of debt is like icing on the cake, huh?"

He smiled placatingly. "I won't say no. This land is a legacy. We'll hand it down for years to come now, and the history that goes with it. John Wesley Hardin slept in this very house. A Comanche war party raided the ranch and killed one of the cowboys. The cavalry used to bivouac on the bottoms on its way to various campaigns toward the Pasa del Norte and back. Yes, girl, this land is full of history. I'd like your kids to inherit it."

She reached out and lightly touched his wrinkled hand. "I understand that. But marriage seems to be hard enough when you love someone. When you don't . . ."

"But you do," Ben replied knowingly. "I've seen the way you watch him, the way you light up when he comes into a room. He doesn't see it because he's not looking. But the fact that he doesn't want an annulment gives you hope, doesn't it?"

"He doesn't want it for the right reasons," she moaned. "Any woman would suit him, don't you see?"

"No, I don't." He tugged his pocket watch out by its gold chain and looked at it. "And I don't have time to make you see it right now, I'm late. Won't be in for lunch, so don't worry about me. C.C. mentioned he might be in for it, though.''

"I'll be sure I leave him something on the table," she muttered.

"Now, now. Is that any way to treat the man who's getting your worried old father out of debt?''

She grimaced. "I guess not. All right, I'll try to look suitably grateful. Now if you'll excuse me," she added, getting up to stack the dishes, "I've got some chores to do. And I'm not giving up that job, either," she tossed over her shoulder. "If they hire me, I'm going!''

Ben threw up his hands and went toward the door.

Pepi did the dishes and cleaned the house. All the while she was thinking about C.C.'s impromptu invitation to come out to the loading docks and watch them process the new heifers. He'd probably be through long before lunch, and he hadn't pressed his invitation. But she went, anyway, riding lazily down the unpaved ranch road toward the loading docks; the wooden chutes down which arriving cattle were driven into the ranch's only fenced pasture.

As she rode, her mind was comparing this valley land with the mostly desert country farther to the northwest, toward El Paso. The desert country around El Paso was deceptive. Beautiful, in its stark way, and its barren appearance only disguised a multitude of life, animal and plant. The prickly pear cactus could inflict enough hairy thorns to keep a man busy with tweezers and a flashlight for the better part of an hour, but it put forth some of the most elegant blossoms of any desert plant. The rain kindled more blossoms, so that the desert came alive with them. Even the tough mesquite tree put out its own heavenly bloom. Animal life abounded, and not just rattlesnakes and lizards. There were other stretches where

only the creosote bushes grew, spreading like miniature
orchards, with no vegetation nearby because of their
toxic root secretions, which killed any vegetation that
tried to grow up around them. After a rain, their pun-
gent, spicy smell was a treat to the senses. Old pioneers
made medicines and glue out of them.

But where the Mathews ranch sat, near the site of old
Fort Hancock, southeast of El Paso in Hudspeth County,
the Rio Grande was close enough to make the area fer-
tile and there was plenty of grazing land for the cattle.
The U.S. Army had situated a number of forts along the
Rio Grande in the mid and late 1800s in accordance with
the settlement of the southern boundary of Texas against
the Mexican border. The United States accepted respon-
sibility for stopping Indian attacks across the border, so
a number of forts were located along the river. One of
those was Fort Hancock, named for General Winfield
Scott Hancock. Pepi had played on the site of it on trips
with her parents, the eternal history buffs. They'd known
every point of historical interest in the area, which was
why she knew about the Salt War, provoked by the salt
deposit at the base of Guadalupe Peak, which resulted in
some fierce gun battles between people who thought the
salt should be free and others who argued the advantages of private mineral rights. She knew about the Indian hot springs on the Sierra Blanca road, and nearby
Fort Quitman, another of the early forts—although no
real ruins were left of it, only an adobe scale model on
private land.

As a girl, she used to wander around those historic
spots imagining war parties of elegant Comanche war-
riors on horseback—the best light cavalry in the world,
they'd been called. She could imagine men on long cattle drives, and Mexican bandits like Pancho Villa, and

Apache and Yaqui raiders. Her imagination had kept her from brooding about being an only child.

Pepi wondered if C.C. liked history. She'd never asked him. She frowned as the mare picked up her pace as they approached the bottoms near what they privately called Mathews Creek, a tributary of the Rio Grande. This area was known to flood when the spring rains came, otherwise it was the haunt of such creatures as pronghorn antelope and white-tailed deer. Her father occasionally allowed hunting on his land, but only if he knew the people involved. Since man had killed off most of the predators that once kept the browsing animals in check, man now had to arrange a less natural way of reducing the number of antelope and deer. Otherwise they overgrazed the land and threatened the survival of the cattle and even themselves.

She felt her heart climb into her throat when she saw the big trucks still unloading new stock, because C.C. was straddling the fence supervising the operation. He must have sensed her approach, because he looked straight at her. Even at the distance, she could see the smile.

He jumped down from the fence and moved toward her, lean and rangy and dangerous. She wondered if there had ever been a man like him. He was certainly the stuff her dreams were made of.

"So you decided to join us," he mused. "Well, come on down."

She swung out of the saddle and fell into step beside him, the reins loosely in her hand. The mare followed noisily behind them.

"That's a lot of cattle," she mentioned when they'd tied the mare to the fence a little farther along.

He glanced down at her. "It takes a lot of cattle to make a living these days," he reminded her. "Especially for ranchers like your father and me, who aren't taking shortcuts."

She frowned. "Shortcuts?"

"Hormone implants, super vitamins, that kind of thing."

"Didn't I read in Dad's market bulletin that some foreign countries were refusing to import cattle with hormone implants that make them grow faster and bigger?" she asked.

He grinned. "Did your homework, I see," he mused. He lit a cigarette and pushed back the brim of his battered tan Stetson. "That's right. People are becoming more health conscious. We have to raise leaner beef in more natural ways to fit the market. Even the pesticides we use on our grain is under fire."

"Not to mention branding," she murmured, darting a glance upward.

"Don't get me started," he began gently. "It isn't cruel, but it is necessary. A freeze-dried brand won't last or be visible after a year or so. Even a burnt brand fades after the cattle shed their coats a few times. Ear tags can be removed. Hot branding is the only way a rancher can protect his investment and mark his cattle. Anything less is an open invitation to rustlers to come and wipe us out."

"I can hear the giggles now. Rustlers, in the space age."

"You know as well as I do that rustling is big business, even if they do it with trucks instead of box canyons," he muttered. "Damn it, we're under the gun from every side these days. People may have to choose between meat and tubes of food paste one day, but until they're willing to pass up a juicy steak, some concessions are going to have to be made."

"I still don't think they ought to torture animals unnecessarily," she said doggedly. "Not just out of curiosity, or to make cosmetics safer for women."

He chuckled. "You and your soft heart. You'd make pets of all my steers and name the chickens, wouldn't you? A hundred years ago you'd have starved to death. And I'll remind you of a time when children died by the thousands or were crippled by endless diseases. How do you think the researchers found cures for those diseases?"

"By using animals for their experiments, I guess," she said uneasily.

"Damned straight. And a hundred years ago, if you couldn't kill an animal, you starved." He stared out over the range. "Cruelty is a part of life. Like it or not, you and I are predators, animals. Man is just a savage with the edges smoothed over. Put him in a primitive environment with an empty belly, and he'll kill every time."

"Can we talk about something less violent?" she asked. "Are your brothers like you?"

He turned, staring down at her appreciatively, from her loosened reddish hair to her rounded figure in jeans. "Evan is," he said finally. "He's the eldest. We look alike, although he's more reserved than I am. Harden is closest to my age, but he's blue-eyed. My youngest brother is Donald—he got married just before I left to come here. Nice girl. Her name is Jo Ann."

"Are your parents still alive?" she asked.

"Our father died when we were just boys. Mother's still around, though." He hooked his thumbs in his wide leather belt and looked down at Pepi. "Her name is Theodora," he said, his gaze falling to Pepi's mouth. "If we have a daughter, I'd like to name her after my mother. She's a special woman. Gritty and capable and loving. She'd like you, Penelope Mathews Tremayne."

She felt her face going hot. He was much too close, and the threat of that lean, fit body made her nervous. She shifted away a little, but he moved with her, his smile telling her that he knew very well how he affected her.

"I'm not a Tremayne for long," she said defensively.

"For as long as I say so, you are," he murmured. "Marriage isn't something to be taken lightly. If you didn't want to marry me, you should never have let me convince you to do into that Mexican wedding chapel."

He had a point there, but she couldn't admit it. She stuck her hands into her pockets to keep them still. She couldn't get her eyes up past his shirt. It was blue-checked, Western cut, and drawn taut across that broad expanse of chest. She could see the shadow of hair under it. She'd seen him without his shirt once or twice, but only from a distance. She couldn't help wonder what he looked like up close, and when she realized what she was thinking, her face flamed.

He lifted an eyebrow. "My, my, aren't we unsettled?" he mused with a slow smile. "Want me to take it off, Pepi?" he drawled softly.

Her eyes shot up to his, glanced off them and darted away to the cattle. Her heart almost shook her with its beat and her mouth went bone-dry as she searched for poise. "I was...admiring the color," she stammered.

"You were undressing me, you mean," he said casually, lifting the cigarette to his mouth. "Why don't you?" he murmured. "We're married. I don't mind if you touch me."

She actually gasped and started to move away, but he caught a long strand of her hair between his hard fingers and stayed the movement effectively.

"Don't run from me," he said, his voice deep and slow, carrying even over the bawling of the cattle and the shouts of the nearby cowboys who were unloading them. A big cattle trailer had been backed in, shielding them from the men with its bulk. "It's time you faced up to the reality of our situation."

"Our situation would resolve itself if you'd agree to an annulment." She choked out the words.

His hand moved, tangling in her hair. He turned her, lifted her face to his with the pressure of it, and his dark eyes had an odd, new glint in their narrowed depths. "Annulments are for people who can't work out their problems. You and I are going to give this marriage a chance, starting now, here."

"We're what . . . C.C.!"

His mouth covered her startled cry. He didn't relent, even when she twisted and tried to fight him. He threw the cigarette in the dirt and his free arm gathered her up against the length of his hard-muscled, fit body. The warm strength of it weakened her will. Slowly she became aware of her hands gripping his muscular arms frantically, her breathing almost stifled. Then she began to feel the slow warmth of his mouth against her own, the sensual movements growing gentler and more insistent by the second.

Brandon had kissed her. So had other boys. But it had been nothing like this. She barely felt the hot sun on her head or heard the noise around them or smelled the dust. She hesitated in her struggles for an instant and gave in to the steely arm around her back. He moved her closer, and she shivered a little with the newness of letting a man hold her like this, in an embrace that was nothing short of intimate.

His mouth lifted, brushed, touched the corners of hers as he felt her resistance slackening. She melted into him unexpectedly and his cheek drew slowly against hers, lifting fractionally so that he could see her eyes. The dazed pleasure in them made him hungry. Soft, pale darkness under those long, thick lashes, pierced with curiosity and need.

"The . . . men," she managed halfheartedly.

He turned her just fractionally, so that she could see that they were shielded from view by the cattle trailer. "What men, little one?" he whispered. His mouth settled on hers like the brush of a butterfly's wing. Lifted. Teased. "Slide your arms under mine," he murmured as he nibbled her lower lip. "Come close."

She obeyed him helplessly, sinking into a sweet oblivion that throbbed with new sensations. Her hands flattened against his shoulder blades. Odd, she thought dazedly, how well they fit together, despite his superior height.

"Kiss me, Mrs. Tremayne," he whispered, coaxing her lips apart.

She went under. His mouth was gentle, and then not gentle. She moaned as the pressure and insistence grew to shocking hunger, and she felt her legs begin to tremble against the hard pressure of his.

He let her go unexpectedly and drew back, his jaw clenched, his eyes strange and glittery. "Wrong time, wrong place," he said huskily. He took a slow breath and surveyed his handiwork, nodded as he saw the unmistakable signs of arousal. "Yes, you want me," he said under his breath. "That's a start, at least."

She swallowed. Her lips felt bruised and when she closed them, she tasted him. She wanted to ask him why, but he took her hand and tugged, pulling her along with him.

"These are Herefords," he said as if nothing at all had happened. "You know that we cross Brahman cattle with shorthorns to produce Santa Gertrudis. Well, this is another kind of cross," he said, and proceeded to give her a refresher course in cattle breeding.

She listened, but her eyes were all over his face, and her body was burning.

He lit a cigarette while he talked, and once he smiled down at her in a way that made her heart beat heavily. They seemed to have crossed some new bridge, quite unexpectedly, and she felt a sense of excitement that she'd never anticipated. Even when he had to leave her to go back to work, and she was riding home again on the mare, the excitement lingered. She only wished she knew where they were headed together.

As she gazed at him, drinking in his sharp features, his dark complexion and lithe, muscular build, she wondered what a child of theirs would look like.

The thought embarrassed her and she dragged her eyes away. There would be plenty of time for that kind of curiosity later, if and when things worked out between them.

Chapter Eight

Life got more complicated very quickly. Brandon came by to see Pepi the next morning, a little hesitant because she was still technically married to C.C. Brandon didn't quite understand what was going on. Pepi had told him that the marriage was a mistake, but C.C. was glaring daggers at him from across the living-room coffee table, and he felt like a buck under the sights of a marksman.

"I, uh, thought we might take in a movie tomorrow night, that is, if C.C. doesn't mind," Brandon added quickly.

Pepi hadn't seen C.C. until Brandon showed up, but here he sat, self-appointed chaperon, and the way he was watching Brandon made her nervous.

C.C. leaned back in his chair and smoked his cigarette with arrogant self-confidence. "Pepi is my wife," he told the younger man. "I don't think married ladies should date other men. Just a little quirk of mine," he added with faintly dangerous eyes.

Brandon's eyes widened. "I thought...Pepi said," he faltered, glancing at her and finding no help, "that it was all a mistake."

"It might have started that way," C.C. replied. "But Pepi and I are determined to make the most of our unfortunate situation. Aren't we, Penelope?"

She looked at him uncertainly. She hadn't felt like herself since the day before, when C.C. had kissed her with such passion. He was backing her into a corner, and she couldn't see the way out.

"Now, look here, C.C.," she began.

He smiled at her lazily. "Connal, sweetheart, remember? Her memory comes and goes, poor little squirt," he told Brandon.

"It does not!" she raged at him. "I never forget anything!"

"Just a few minutes ago, you forgot you were married." He shrugged. "Can't blame a man for worrying when his own wife forgets her own wedding."

Pepi fumed while Brandon shifted uncomfortably in the chair. He looked as if his world was coming down around his ears. "I wanted to have another look at those two heifers with the parasites," he told C.C., changing the subject. "How are those calves that we're treating for scours?"

"They're better," the older man replied. "But I'd feel easier if we had more time to watch them. We've had a lot of sick cattle. I don't like it."

"Might not hurt to check the graze," Brandon suggested. "They may be getting into something toxic."

"I had the same idea." C.C. nodded. "I'm going to have those tanks checked today, too. There may be something leaching into the water supply."

"Just thank your lucky stars we aren't up near the Guadalupe Mountains, where the salt flats are," Brandon murmured dryly.

"I do, every day." C.C. got to his feet. "I'll walk you out. We've got company coming today, so I don't have a lot of time to spare. I'll let Darby go with you to see about the calves."

Pepi didn't like the expression on his face. She jumped up. "I'll go, too."

C.C. lifted an eyebrow, but he didn't say anything. Pepi went out behind Brandon, who was looking more than a little flustered.

They walked toward the barn, where Darby, the wizened little wrangler, was working. C.C. left Brandon with him and came back to where Pepi was waiting and watching. He took her arm and led her around the corner of the house, where his Ford sat by the deserted bunkhouse a few hundred yards from the back barn.

"Where are we going?" she asked.

"To the airport to meet my brothers, have you forgotten?" he asked conversationally.

"Yes, I guess I had," she said. "But I didn't know I was going with you to get them," she added meaningfully. "I'm not properly dressed...."

"You look fine to me," he murmured, his eyes approving the long denim skirt she was wearing with her high-topped moccasins and a pullover knit blouse. "I like your hair down like that."

"Does it really matter how I wear it?" she asked coolly. "After all, it won't make me any less fat."

His breath stilled. He caught her hand and turned her toward him, his black eyes quiet and steady on her face. "I regret saying that most of all," he told her, "because you please me exactly the way you are. I wanted to hurt you." He looked down at her small hand in his. "God help me, I said things I never meant to. It was a shock, and not a very pleasant one at the time. I didn't know the circumstances, if that's any excuse. I don't expect you to get over it very soon. But maybe the wounds will heal in time. I have to hope so, Pepi."

Her pale brown eyes fell to his thin, sensuous mouth and lifted again to meet his eyes. "We were friends," she began. "I wish we could be again."

"Do you?" He moved a little closer, his expression as much a threat as his taut, fit body. "After yesterday, I doubt either of us is going to be able to settle for just friendship." His eyes fell to her soft mouth. "I want you."

She moved back a step, her face mirroring her indecision. "You want Edie, too."

He frowned. "In the same way you wanted Hale?" he probed suspiciously. "Some suitor, rushing out the door without you. I'd have laid my head open with a stick and taken you off to safety if I'd been him."

"I'd like to see you lay your own head open with a stick," she muttered.

He chuckled. "That wasn't what I meant." He lifted his chin and, with one eye narrowed, he looked down his nose at her. "Did you want him, little one?" he asked very softly. He let go of her hand and lifted his, knuckles down, to her collarbone. He trailed it slowly over the fabric, the sound of it loud in the stillness of early morning, his eyes assessing her sudden color, the rustle of her breath.

"C.C...." she whispered uncertainly, but she didn't try to move away.

"It's all right," he said quietly. "I'm your husband."

She couldn't think, which was just as well. The back of his hand moved down ever further, over the knit blouse to the swell of her breast—back and forth with delicate tenderness, until she felt as if her whole body was on fire. Her breath caught in her throat; she was burning with need.

As if he sensed her hunger, his forefinger bent and he brushed it down to her nipple, making it go suddenly hard and exquisitely sensitive. She gasped audibly.

He saw the heat in her cheeks and felt her faint shudder with a sense of shocking satisfaction.

"It was a lie," he said curtly. "You haven't had Hale. You haven't had a man at all."

She couldn't deny it. But she couldn't move, either. He was casting a spell over her. She loved the pleasure his touch was giving. She was getting drunk on it, in fact.

He glanced around them, frustrated and hungry to teach her more than this cursory lesson, but there were damned cowboys everywhere, coming out of the woodwork, and any minute they were going to be heading for that back barn. His brothers were due in thirty minutes. He wanted to throw something.

He looked back down at Pepi, his hard face showing new lines. "This will have to do, for now," he said huskily. He slid his free hand under the thick fall of her hair and lifted her mouth. "God, it hurts . . . !" he groaned.

She didn't understand. His mouth settled on hers in soft, teasing movements and his hand went slowly under her breast to lift its soft weight while his thumb slid roughly over the taut nipple.

"Oh!" she groaned against his mouth, but it wasn't pain that dragged the sound out of her, and he knew it.

"Open your mouth," he ground out at her lips.

She fit her lips to his and lifted her arms around him, shivering, trying to get closer to that expert hand on her breast. But all at once, he moved both hands to her hips and jerked.

Her shocked exclamation went into his mouth. He moved her thighs in a quick, sharp rotation against his aroused body and then put her away from him just as roughly.

"No," he said shortly when she tried, dazed, to move back into his arms. "Come on," he said, catching her arm to pull her along with him toward the car.

His hand was rough on her soft flesh, but she hardly felt it. She was shaking all over. So that was what it felt like to make love. She was sure there was a lot more to it, like having their clothes out of the way. Her skin went hot and she sighed huskily at the thought of C.C.'s lean, hard hands on her naked body.

"Miss Experience," he bit off, glaring down at her. "My God, why did you lie to me?"

"I thought it would make me less vulnerable," she said without thinking.

His eyes darted from her swollen, parted lips back up to her shocked face. "You look less vulnerable, all right," he said mockingly.

"You needn't make fun of me, C.C.," she whispered. "I can't help the way you make me feel."

He opened the passenger door of the Ford and stood aside to let her get in. "I'm not making fun of you," he replied. "If you want the truth, it arouses me like hell to have you cave in when I touch you."

She looked up at him, her pale brown eyes curious and a little afraid. He seemed very adult and worlds ahead of her in experience. "What you . . . did to me," she asked hesitantly, trying not to stammer. "Does it feel like that, in bed?"

His heart stopped beating. Then it went wild, and his body strung him out. He searched her soft eyes in a silence that throbbed with promise.

"Why don't you come to me tonight, and I'll show you?" he asked quietly.

Her eyes widened until the pupils seemed to blot out their color. "You mean... sleep with you?" she whispered.

He nodded. "The bunkhouse is empty, now that we're through roundup. You're my wife," he added, feeling the words all the way to his toes. "There's no shame in it, Pepi," he added when he saw her hesitation. "It would only be the consummation of our wedding vows." He lifted her hand and drew its palm hungrily to his lips. "Until you sleep with me," he added huskily, "we're not legally married. Did you know that?"

"No. I mean, no, I didn't," she faltered. The look in his eyes was melting her ankles. She could hardly stand up. It was hard to remember that he didn't love her. She had to try to keep that in mind, but it was difficult to keep anything in mind with his eyes piercing hers like that.

"Afraid of it?" he asked quietly.

"Yes, a little," she whispered.

"I'll be careful with you." He drew her hand to his chest and pressed it there, palm down, so that she could feel the powerful beating of his heart under his shirt.

"It will hurt," she blurted out.

"Maybe," he agreed. "But you won't care."

She searched his eyes curiously.

"You may find bruises on your hips tomorrow because I was rough with you on the way here," he replied, his voice deep and slow. "I didn't intend to be that rough, but you were fighting to get back into my arms afterward, not to get out of them."

Her lips parted. She'd forgotten the steely bite of his fingers into her soft flesh. "So it's like that," she whispered.

"Yes. It's like that. A fever that burns so wild and so high, you can't even feel pain through it." His face hardened. "I'll make you so damned hungry for me that you won't care what I do to you."

"But, what about Edie...." she whispered painfully.

He framed her face in his hands and bent to kiss her forehead with breathless tenderness. "Edie was a pleasant, and a very innocent, diversion," he whispered, sliding his cheek against hers so that his breath was warm at her ear. "I haven't slept with her."

"But ... you must have wanted to," she began again.

He lifted his head, and his dark eyes searched hers slowly. "Pepi, I don't really understand why, but maybe the guilt made it difficult for me to deal with relationships. I...haven't wanted sex since Marsha died. At least, not until yesterday."

"You wanted me," she whispered with growing wonder.

"Oh, yes, I did," he said with undisguised hunger. "I still do, more every day." His eyes slid down her body and he drew her against him, his lean hands on her shoulders. "Do you want to give me a baby?" he asked.

It was the first time anyone had asked her that. She felt her body burning with heat, and she knew her freckles were standing out like crazy in her face. "Now?" she asked uncertainly.

"If you don't want to get pregnant, I'll have to do something to prevent it," he explained gently.

"Oh." She averted her eyes. "Well, I...I don't know." Things were moving fast. Almost too fast. She felt hunted.

"Don't look like that," he said, his voice almost tender as he tipped her face up to his eyes. "You don't have to, if you don't want to. I'm in no hurry. We've got the rest of our lives. If you want to spend some time getting used to me first, that's all right. I'll never rush you."

"C.C.," she said softly, and she smiled at him. "You're a nice man."

"That's what I've been trying to tell you. It's just that I haven't quite tried to prove it, yet," he added with a smile full of self-mockery. "And my name is Connal."

"Yes. Connal." She reached up hesitantly and paused, but he caught her fingers and drew them to his face, letting her trace his dark eyebrows, his straight nose, the hard curve of his thin mouth.

"We'll take one day at a time," he assured her solemnly. "No pressure."

"Thank you."

He smiled and put her in the car, sliding in beside her with apparent good humor to start the engine.

She fastened her seat belt and studied his profile hungrily. "Connal?" she asked.

He glanced at her and lifted an eyebrow.

"Do you . . . I mean, is a child important to you?" she asked quietly.

He frowned. She made it seem as if he wanted her because she could bear him one. He wasn't certain what to say to reassure her. She'd said that she wasn't in love with him, although she was certainly attracted to him. God knew, he didn't want to frighten her off.

"Eventually, yes," he compromised. "Don't you want children?"

"Yes, I do," she said huskily, meeting his eyes. "I want them very much."

His chest began to swell. He hoped against hope that someday she'd want them because she loved him. But it would take time, he reminded himself. He mustn't be impatient.

He didn't say anything else. He nodded and turned his attention back to the road.

The airport was crowded, and Pepi clung to C.C.'s lean hand on the way through the crush of people.

"Everybody decided to come on the same day," he mused, moving aside with her to let the embarking passengers get by. For a brief moment, they were alone in the corridor. He chuckled and drew her along with him, his spurs "making music" as the cowboys like to call it.

"I'd forgotten what spurs sounded like," she murmured.

"I forgot to take them off this morning," he recalled. "Back in the old days, the Mexican spurs were so big that vaqueros had to take them off just to walk," he replied. "God knows how their mounts survived."

"You use spurs when you help break horses," she reminded him.

He smiled down at her. "Sure I do. But you know we use special spurs that don't break the skin or injure the horse's hide. To a horse, it's like being tickled. That's why he jumps and sunfishes."

Her hand felt very small and helpless in his. It wasn't a feeling she'd have liked with another man, but with C.C. it seemed very natural.

She looked down, marking the size of her foot and his. He had big feet, too, but they suited him because he was so tall.

"I don't have big feet," he remarked, accurately reading her mind.

"Did I say anything?" she protested.

He chuckled. "You didn't have to. There they are!" he said suddenly, looking over the crowd in front of them. "Evan! Harden!"

Two men who looked very much like C.C. moved toward them. They weren't wearing working clothes, though. They were in suits. The taller man had on a pearl-gray vested suit with a matching Stetson. He was huskily built, but certainly not overweight. He looked like a wrestler, with dark eyes and dark hair and complexion that was even darker than C.C.'s. The other man was only fractionally shorter, dressed in dark slacks with a white open-necked shirt with a sports jacket. He wore a black Stetson at a cocky angle over his equally black hair, and when he came closer, Pepi noticed that his eyes were a pale, glittery blue under thick black lashes. He had a leaner look than Evan, and a wiry frame that was probably deceptive, because he looked as fit as C.C.

C.C. greeted his brothers and then drew them to where Pepi stood waiting awkwardly, her uncertainty evident in her nervous face.

"Evan, Harden, this is my wife, Penelope," C.C. introduced her, sliding a casual but possessive arm around her shoulders.

"She looks just the way you described her," Harden murmured dryly, extending a lean hand. His pale blue eyes assessed her and gave nothing away. "You're a rancher's daughter, I gathered."

Penelope nodded. "I grew up around horses and cattle," she said quietly, and smiled nervously. "Hereford cattle, of course," she added. "I guess our stock will look pretty mangy to you by comparison with your purebred Santa Gerts."

"Oh, we're not snobs," Harden murmured. He stuck his hands deep in his pockets and glanced at C.C. "Except when it comes to Old Man Red."

"The foundation sire of our herd," Evan added. He extended a hand the size of a plate and shook Pepi's with firm gentleness. His dark eyes narrowed. "You look threatened. No need. We're domesticated, and we've had our shots."

Pepi's rigid stance relaxed and she laughed, her whole face lighting up. Evan didn't smile, but his dark eyes did, and she felt at home for the first time.

"Speak for yourself," Harden drawled, and his blue eyes were briefly cold. "The day I get domesticated you can bury me."

"Harden is a card-carrying bachelor," Evan mused.

"Look who's talking," Harden replied.

"Not my fault that women can't appreciate my superior good looks and charm," the eldest Tremayne shrugged. "They trample me trying to get to you."

Pepi laughed with pure delight. They were nothing like she'd imagined.

"Come on. You can fight out at the ranch," C.C. said. He took Pepi's arm.

"Pity you had to walk off with Penelope before she got a look at us," Evan said, shaking his head. "I'm a much better proposition, Pepi. I still have all my own teeth."

"That's true," Harden agreed. "But only because you knocked out two of Connal's."

"Fair trade," Connal returned. "I got three of his."

"It was a long time ago," Evan said. "We've all calmed down a lot since then."

"C.C. hasn't been very calm lately," Pepi murmured. "I thought he was going to murder me when he found out we were married."

"Served him right for getting drunk," Evan said curtly. "Mother would lay a tire tool across his head for that."

"Oh, Pepi threatened to," C.C. chuckled. "Still a tee-totaller, I see, Evan?"

"He carries it to sickening extremes," Harden murmured. "Justin and Shelby Ballenger will never invite him to another dinner party. He actually got up from the table and carried the glass of wine the waiter accidentally poured back to the kitchen."

C.C. burst out laughing. "Well, Justin never was much of a drinker himself, as I recall. Not in Calhoun's league, anyway."

"Calhoun's gotten as bad as Evan," Harden told him. "He doesn't want to set a poor example for the kids, or so he says."

"Alcohol is a curse," Evan said as they reached the car.

"My father will love you," Pepi said, grinning up at him.

When they got to the ranch, Ben seemed to take to Evan even before he knew about the eldest brother's temperance stance. But he was less relaxed with Harden. In fact, so was Pepi. The blue-eyed brother moved lazily and talked lazily, but Pepi sensed deep, dark currents in him.

The men talked business while Pepi whipped up a quick lunch, but the brothers only stayed for two hours and had to catch a plane right back to Jacobsville. Pepi didn't ride with C.C. to take them to the airport, though. She had a call from her prospective employer just as they were going out the door, and she waved them on to take it.

The insurance company's receptionist had decided that she did want her old job back. They were very apologetic, and promised to let Pepi know the minute they had another opening. She was disheartened, but it was probably just as well.

"We're going to get a bull." Ben Mathews was all but dancing as he told her. "One of the new crop of young bulls out of Checker. Remember reading about him in the trade paper? He's one of the finest herd sires in years!"

"And his progeny cost plenty, I don't doubt," Pepi said. "C.C.'s going to fund the addition, I gather."

"He's a full partner," Ben reminded her. "And we're all in this to make the ranch pay, aren't we?"

"Yes, I guess we are. How do you like his brothers?"

"Oh, Evan's a card. He's very obviously the financial brains of the outfit. Knows his figures."

"And Harden?" she added.

He sat down in his chair and crossed his legs. "Harden is a driven man. I don't know why, but he strikes me as a bad man to have for an enemy. He's charming, but underneath it, there's a darkness of spirit."

"A deep kind of pain," Pepi nodded, "and a terrible anger."

"Exactly. I hope we'll be doing most of our business with Evan. He's more like C.C."

"He's more like two of C.C.," Pepi laughed. "I wonder what the other brother looks like, the one who's married?"

"Just like C.C. and Evan, from what I gather. Harden's the odd one, with those blue eyes. He doesn't really favor the others very much."

"Probably a throwback to another generation, like Aunt Mattie who had dark-haired parents and was a blonde."

"No doubt."

"My job didn't come through," she said after a minute. "They don't need me."

"Then why don't you do some bookkeeping and typing for the ranch?" Ben asked. "Connal said we're going to have to keep proper books now, and there'll be a lot of correspondence. He was going to hire somebody, but you're a good typist and you aren't bad with figures. We can keep it in the family."

"I guess I could," she said. "I like typing."

"You can talk to Connal when he gets back."

She cleaned up the kitchen and made an apple pie. By the time she took it out of the oven, Connal had returned.

"Did they get off all right?" she asked him.

"Like clockwork." He paused by the counter where she was placing a cloth over the pie. "For supper?" he asked hopefully.

She smiled at him shyly. "Yes. I like your brothers," she said.

"They liked you, too. Evan was particularly impressed."

"Evan is easier to get along with. Harden..." She hesitated. "He's...different."

"More different than you know," he said quietly. He moved closer, taking a strand of her hair in his fingers and twirling it around one. "How about supper and a movie tonight?"

"I have to get supper for Dad," she said, hesitating.

"We'll take him with us," he chuckled.

"On a date?" She lifted her eyebrows. "He'd love that. Besides, this is his checkers night with old man Dill down the road. No, I'll fix something for him before we go. He won't mind."

"If you're sure." He sighed heavily, watching her. "Pepi, how would you feel about moving into a house with me?" he added, frowning.

"But . . . but what about Dad?" she asked.

"Consuelo can cook and clean for him. She could go on salary. And there's a house, the Dobbs house. They moved back East last month," he reminded her. "Your father was renting them the house. It's small, but it would be just right for the two of us."

She couldn't cope with so much at once. Things were happening with lightning speed, and her mind was whirling.

"You mean, live with you all the time," she faltered. "Even at night?"

"That's the general idea," he replied. "A wife's place is with her husband."

"You didn't want a wife. You said so . . ."

". . . with alarming repetition, yes, I know," he finished for her. "Will you try to understand that I've changed my mind? That marriage is no longer the terror it was for me?"

"Well, yes, I'll try. But you didn't have much choice about ours, did you?"

He let go of her hair. "Not much," he agreed. "But looking back, I wouldn't have wanted to marry anyone. Surely you realized that?"

"You were pretty adamant about it," she nodded. "I just wish we'd gone about things in the normal way. I'll always feel that you were trapped into a relationship you really didn't want."

"So were you," he replied. "But the thing we have to do now is make the most of it. An annulment would disgrace us both, Pepi, especially your father. Now that he and I are in partnership, the best way to cement it is to make the marriage a real one."

"Is it what you really want, Connal?" she asked worriedly.

"Of course it is," he said.

She couldn't help feeling that he was only saying that to put her at ease. It would hurt his pride to get an annulment. People might think he wasn't enough of a man to fulfill his wedding vows. Too, he might still have in mind using her to ward off other contenders for his hand in marriage.

"Could I have a little more time?" she asked hesitantly.

He stared down at her. After the afternoon, he'd thought she'd be immediately receptive to his advances, but perhaps she'd had too much time to think and she'd gotten cold feet. The last thing he could afford to do was to rush her.

"Okay," he said after a minute. "You can have a little more time. But you and I are going to start doing things together, Pepi. If we don't live together, we're at least going to start acting like married people in public."

"That's all right with me," she said. But afterward, she worried about Edie. Had Connal told her about his marriage? And was his relationship with Edie really as innocent as he'd said it was?

Chapter Nine

Connal took her to the same exclusive restaurant in El Paso where she'd gone with Brandon the night before her father's birthday. She was wearing a plain gray jersey dress with a pretty scarf, her hair down around her shoulders, and Connal had told her that she looked delightfully pretty. Even if he was lying, it was exciting to go on a real date with him, to have his dark eyes possessive on her face as they walked to their table.

He looked elegant in a dinner jacket and dark slacks, his white silk shirt a perfect foil for his dark complexion and darker eyes and hair. Pepi loved to look at him. She thought that in all the world, there couldn't be a more handsome man.

He seated her and then himself, and she smiled at him until a movement caught her eye and she saw Edie sitting at a nearby table all alone, staring pointedly at Connal.

"I'd better have a word with her," he told Pepi, his eyes narrowing. "I won't be a minute."

He got up and went to the other table, smiling at an Edie who became suddenly radiant. The blonde was wearing a simple black sheath dress cut almost to the navel in front, and Pepi despaired of the way she probably compared to the sophisticated older woman.

She couldn't tear her eyes away from them. They did look so right together, and despite C.C.'s determination to make the most of a bad situation—their marriage—she felt guilty and ashamed that he'd had to be trapped into marrying her when he'd have been so much better off with Edie. Pepi was just a country girl. She had no sophistication. She didn't even know how to choose the kind of clothes that were proper for a place like this. Inevitably she was going to be a dismal disappointment for a man like Connal, who was born to wealth and high society.

Edie's face suddenly went rigid. She stared at Pepi blankly for an instant, and then with quickly concealed rage. Her attention went back to C.C. and she seemed to come apart emotionally. She started crying.

C.C. got her up out of her chair and put a comforting arm around her as he led her gently out of the restaurant.

Obviously he'd told her about the marriage. Did he tell her, Pepi wondered, that it had been a forced one, and not of his choosing? Was he going to take her home now or get her a cab?

Ten minutes passed and Pepi grew more upset as she realized he'd more than likely driven Edie home. He'd comfort her, surely. Maybe more than that. He and Edie were close, even if they weren't lovers. Or had he stretched the truth about that, too?

The waiter hovered and Pepi went ahead and ordered soup du jour and a chef's salad. It was all she had any appetite for.

She'd just finished when C.C. came back, his expression telling her nothing as he sat down across from her.

"Is she all right?" Pepi asked quietly.

"Not really, but she'll do. I should have picked a better place to tell her," he said shortly. "God, I never expected that kind of reaction."

"She's been your only steady date for a long time," Pepi said with downcast eyes. "It's understandable that she had hopes of her own."

C.C. hated scenes. It brought back unpleasant memories of times when Marsha had put away too many cocktails and did her best to embarrass him. She'd never succeeded. Neither had Edie, but it touched off his temper.

"Women always have hopes," he said with cold bitterness. "Of course, not all of them are fortunate enough to catch a man drunk and drag him into a Mexican wedding chapel."

Pepi closed her eyes. She shouldn't let him get to her like this. Despite his ardor, his desire for her, underneath there was always going to be resentment that he'd been less than sober when he signed the marriage license. He was never going to let Pepi forget, either, and what kind of life was that going to be for either of them?

"I wouldn't exactly call it fortunate," Pepi replied without looking at him.

"Thank you," he replied acidly. "I can return the compliment."

The waiter came and C.C. ordered a steak and salad. He sipped the coffee he'd ordered and glared at Pepi. It wasn't her fault, he knew, but he was furious at Edie's theatrics and Pepi's meek acceptance of his bad humor. He wanted a fight, and he couldn't seem to start one. If Pepi continued to knuckle under like this, marriage was going to be impossible for her.

"Nothing to say?" he prodded.

She tightened her fingers around the water glass. "What would you like to hear?" She lifted the glass, her pale brown eyes glittering with dislike. "Or would you prefer something nonverbal but just as enlightening?"

His eyes began to twinkle. "Go ahead. Throw it."

She glanced around at the elegant diners surrounding them and thought better of it. There were some priceless antiques decorating the place. With her luck she'd hit something irreplaceable and land them in debt for years. She put the water glass down.

"It's not my fault," she said coldly. "You're the one who threatened to shoot up Juárez."

"And you knew I didn't have a gun," he countered.

"No, I didn't," she returned. "Dad told me once that you have a Beretta and a license to carry it. I had no way of knowing there wasn't one in your pocket, and I wasn't about to frisk you."

"God forbid," he said with mock horror. "Imagine having to touch a live man like *that*!"

"Cut it out," she muttered, reddening.

"You are a greenhorn and a half, aren't you?" he mused. "Don't know how to kiss, don't know how to make love, wouldn't dream of touching a man below the belt..."

"Stop!" She glanced around quickly to make sure nobody had heard him, her face beet-red. "Somebody might hear you!"

"So what? We're married." His eyes narrowed. "Till death do us part," he added mockingly.

Her own eyes narrowed and she smiled sweetly. "In that case, do check your bed at night, dear man. I'll see if I can find a couple of rattly bedmates for you."

"One of your ranch hands did that, the first night I was here," he recalled, grinning at her shock. "Didn't they ever tell you?"

"Somebody put a live rattlesnake in your bed?" she gasped.

"Indeed they did," he replied. "Fortunately they'd defanged him first, but it was an interesting experience."

"What did you do?"

"You didn't hear the gunshot, either, I gather?" he mused.

"You shot it?"

"Uh-huh," he agreed. "Right through the head, the mattress, and the bunkhouse floor."

"Poor old snake," she said.

He gave her a hard glare. "Aren't you the one who leaped up onto the hood of a truck from a standing start when one came slithering past your foot this summer?"

"I didn't say I liked them," she emphasized. "But I think it's horrible to kill things without reason. What could the poor thing have done to you—gummed you to death?"

"You're forgetting I didn't know he'd had his fangs pulled."

"Oh. I guess not."

The waiter brought his meal and he ate it in silence, noticing that Pepi's eyes wandered back to the window and the sharp, dark outline of the mountains in the distance. She was brooding, and he felt bad that he'd attacked her without reason.

"I suppose Edie was angry?" she said, fishing.

He finished the last bit of his steak and washed it down with steaming black coffee. "That's an understatement. She had a lot to say when I told her how our marriage had come about."

"Including advising you on the quickest way to have it annulled, I imagine?" she asked miserably.

"I told her we couldn't get an annulment," he murmured dryly.

"But, of course we can," she said without thinking. "We haven't—" She broke off, gasping.

He watched her eyes widen when she realized what he was saying.

"You didn't tell Edie that?" she burst out.

"Why not?" His black eyes probed hers. "Regardless of how they got said, I consider marriage vows binding. That means I don't have women on the side. As for what we haven't done yet, you'll sleep with me, eventually. You're as hungry for it as I am. Maybe even hungrier. I remember how I ached before my first time. And I wanted Marsha so much that I couldn't sleep at night."

Neither could she, but she wasn't about to admit that to him. She lowered her eyes to the table. "I suppose your first wife loved you?" she asked idly.

"She loved the idea of my money, just like the ones who come after her, up to and including Edie," he replied with a cynicism that shocked Pepi. He looked at that moment like a man who'd known every conceivable kind of woman and trusted none of them.

"Did Edie know who you were?" Pepi asked.

He nodded. "Through a mutual friend. So you see, it wasn't love eternal on her part. She enjoyed a good time and eating in the best places. But she'll find someone else. There are plenty of well-heeled bachelors around."

"Are you as cynical as you sound?" she asked.

"Every bit," he replied narrowly. "Even Marsha married me as much for what I have as what I was. She told me she couldn't endure being married to a man who worked for wages. She was pretty and I wanted her. But long before the accident, I regretted marrying her."

Would it be that way with Pepi, too, she wondered. Would he be that resentful of her? He already disliked the way they'd been married.

"You must have missed her, though," she said gently.

"I missed her," he agreed. "I missed the child more. God, it was hard living with that! If I'd had any idea, any idea at all that she was pregnant, I'd never have let her in the raft. But she was too possessive to let me go alone. There were two other women in the rafting party, and she'd convinced herself that I wanted both of them."

She studied his hard face. "Didn't she know that you aren't the kind of man who'd forsake any vow he made?" she said after a minute.

His head came up and his dark eyes glittered into hers. "If you believe that, why did you look so accusing when I came back from taking Edie home? Were you picturing me in bed with her?"

She blushed. "There's a big difference between taking a vow voluntarily and taking one when you're out of your mind on tequila," she said with wan pride. "You didn't get married out of choice, this time." She picked up her napkin and stroked the embossed design. "It's not going to work, C.C.," she added wearily.

"Oh, hell, yes, it is," he said tersely. He finished his coffee. "I'm still in the adjustment stage, that's all. Until recently I thought of you as Ben's tomboy teenage daughter."

So that was it. Probably she still acted like one, too. But it was beyond her abilities to pretend a sophistication she didn't have.

"Or your nursemaid," she mused, smiling a little. "That's what you said in Juárez, that since I was always playing nursemaid, we might as well get married so I'd have an excuse."

"You've always looked out for me," he said quietly. "I never thought of you in a physical way, Pepi. It was as much a shock for me as it was for you that morning in the kitchen when your father interrupted us," he added, his eyes glittery under his thick lashes.

She averted her gaze. She remembered, too. It had been the sexiest kind of lovemaking, but he hadn't even kissed her.

"If things had happened naturally," he continued, his voice deepened, "it wouldn't have affected me the way it did."

"They wouldn't have happened naturally, and you know it, C.C.," she told him, her eyes a little sad as they met his. "You'd never in a million years have wanted somebody like me. I guess if this hadn't come up, you'd have married Edie eventually."

"Didn't you hear a word I just said, about why Edie kept going out with me?" he asked irritably.

"Edie loves you," she muttered. "I'm not blind, even if you're trying to be. She genuinely cared about you. No woman is completely mercenary, and there's a lot more to you than just the size of your wallet."

He lifted an eyebrow. "Really? Name something."

"You're kind," she said, taking the sarcasm at face value. "You don't go out of your way to start fights, but you'll stand your ground when it's necessary. You're fair and open-minded when it counts, and you have a lot of heart.''

He stared at her. ''I thought you didn't care enough about me to want to stay married to me?'' he murmured, touched by her opinion of him.

''And I'll remind you again that you're the one who wanted the annulment and went storming off in a snit to get it,'' she shot back. ''I still don't understand what changed your mind while you were away.''

''Evan did,'' he said after a minute. ''He accused me of running from commitment.'' He paused to light a cigarette, staring absently at his lighter before he repocketed it. ''I guess in a way he was right. I couldn't bear the thought of another Marsha, another possessive woman smothering me. I couldn't bear the thought, either, that tragedy could repeat itself, because I was still working out the guilt I felt over Marsha's death. Evan said that I should keep you, if you were brave enough to take me on,'' he added, staring at her quietly. ''He thought you sounded like exactly the kind of woman I needed. And maybe he was right, Pepi. The last thing you are is possessive.''

She could have laughed out loud at that! Of course she was possessive; she loved him. But he obviously didn't want a woman who cared deeply about him. He wanted a shallow relationship that would allow him to remain heart-free and independent, and she couldn't settle for that.

''All the same, I'm not sure I can handle this,'' Pepi confessed. ''You'll never get over the fact that it was an accidental marriage. Even a few minutes ago, when you were upset about Edie, you threw it up to me.''

"Haven't you been doing the same thing, about what I said to you before I left to visit my brothers in Jacobsville?" he countered.

She shrugged. "I guess I have. But we're two pretty different people, C.C., and I won't ever get used to a rich life-style or high society," she said honestly. "I'm not a social animal."

His face went hard. "You don't think you can live with me as I am?"

"I could have lived very well with my father's foreman, who was just an ordinary working man," she replied. "I'm made for cooking and cleaning, for taking care of a house and raising a family. I'm just not cut out for society bashes, and no matter how hard you try to change me, you'll never get the country out of me."

He lifted his chin, his eyes narrowing on her face. "Do I strike you as the kind of man who lives from party to party?" he asked.

"You've been hiding out for three years," Pepi reminded him, "living a life-style that probably wasn't a patch on the one you left behind. I don't know anything about that side of your life at all."

"Would you like to?" he asked. "We could go to Jacobsville and visit my family for a few days."

She hesitated. Harden intimidated her, but she liked Evan well enough. "What's your mother like?" she asked.

He smiled. "She's like Evan," he replied. "She's dry and capable and easy to like. She'll like you, too."

"Harden doesn't like me," she said.

"Harden doesn't like women, sweetheart," he said gently. "Despite the fact that he's got a face like a dark angel and the charm to match, he's the original woman-hater."

"Then it wasn't just me," she said, a little relieved.

"It wasn't. He hates our mother most of all," he added quietly. "That's why he doesn't live at home. Evan does, because it's too much of a burden for Mother, but Harden has an apartment in Houston, where our offices are located."

She wanted to follow up on that, but it probably wasn't the best time to start probing into family secrets.

"I guess we'd have to stay in the same room?" she asked worriedly.

His dark eyes searched hers in a warm silence. "Yes."

"Twin beds?" she asked hopefully.

He shook his head.

"Oh." She toyed with her fork, going warm all over at the thought of sleeping with him.

"Want to back out?" he challenged softly.

She lifted her eyes to his and hesitated. Then she gave in, all at once. She loved him. If he wanted to try to make their marriage work, this was the first step. He seemed adamant about not getting an annulment, and she didn't really want one, either.

"No," she said. "I don't want to back out."

His face tautened and he seemed to have a hard time breathing. "Brave words," he said huskily. "Suppose I have more in mind than sharing a pillow with you?"

She gnawed on her lower lip. "That's inevitable, isn't it?" she asked hesitantly. "If we stay married, I mean."

He nodded. "I won't settle for a platonic marriage. I want a child, Pepi," he added, his voice deeper, slower as he stared into her eyes.

She stared at her hands, neatly folded in front of her on the table. "I'd like that. I'm just a little nervous about it, that's all. Most women these days are experienced."

"You can't imagine what a rare and exquisite thing a virgin bride is to me," he said quietly. "Your innocence excites me, Pepi. Just thinking about our first time makes my knees go weak."

It made hers go weak, too, but she didn't think she should admit it. Her eyes glanced off his and away again. "When did you plan for us to visit your family?" she asked instead, changing the subject.

"Tomorrow. My mother wants to meet you. It wouldn't hurt to let her see that I haven't let history repeat itself."

"As if you had much choice." She sighed. "Oh, C.C., I'm so sorry I got us into this mess," she groaned, meeting his dark gaze levelly. "I didn't know what to do. Edie or somebody like her could have coped with it better."

"Edie or somebody like her would have been laughing like hell at my predicament and adding up the settlement all at the same time," he replied. "They wouldn't have flayed themselves with attacks of conscience."

"Wouldn't you like to get an annulment, anyway?" she asked him. "Then, you'd have the right to choose…"

"Is it the damned redheaded vet after all?" he shot back, suddenly dark-faced with rage. "Well, is it?"

"What do you mean?" she faltered, staggered by the venom in the attack.

He leaned forward, his eyes like black fires burning in his lean face. "You know what I mean. He's in love with you. Was it mutual? Is he why you're so single-minded about that annulment, so you can dump me and marry him?"

"Brandon did ask me to marry him, but…" she began.

"But you did your Florence Nightingale act and followed me to Juárez," he said angrily. "Well, don't hold your breath until I let you go. We're married, and we're staying married. And I'd better not catch Hale hanging around you, either!''

She gaped at him. ''That's not fair!'' she tossed right back. ''Even if it wasn't a conventional marriage, I take my vows seriously, too!''

''Do you? Prove it,'' he said tersely.

''Prove it?'' she echoed blankly.

''You know where the bunkhouse is,'' he said with a mocking smile.

She averted her angry face. He'd told her that before and she'd refused, asked for time. Now here he was rushing her again, and it felt almost as if he were requesting something horribly immoral. She couldn't help her reticence. She still didn't feel married to him.

''So you still have cold feet?'' he taunted. ''All right, then. Save your pride. But you'll sleep with me when I take you to visit my family. You gave your word.''

''Yes, I know,'' she said huskily. She folded her napkin neatly and laid it beside her plate. ''Could we go now?''

''Of course.'' He got up and pulled out her chair, pausing to look down at her with troubled dark eyes. ''You're going to fight me every step of the way, aren't you?'' he asked deeply. ''You'll never forget the things I said when I found out about the marriage license.''

''It wasn't any surprise, C.C.,'' she replied, looking up at him with quiet pride. ''I always knew I wasn't your type of woman. You even warned me once, that morning I came to make black coffee for you when you were hung over. You said you didn't have anything to give and told me not to break my heart over you. There was no need to worry. My heart isn't breaking.'' That was true. It had already been broken by his cold indifference.

He let out a rough sigh. He'd closed all his doors and now he didn't know how to open them again. All he knew was that if he lost Pepi, there wouldn't be much left of his life.

He paid the bill and led her out to the car. He didn't say anything, driving quickly and efficiently down the long road paralleling the Rio Grande until they were on the turnoff to the ranch. It was wide open country here, and deserted most all the time.

Pepi sat beside him in a rigid silence, toying with her purse. There was a tension between them that disturbed her. Despite his apparent unconcern as he drove, smoking his cigarette without talking, she sensed that he was boiling underneath. Maybe Edie had upset him and he couldn't get over having lost her. She didn't take his remarks about Brandon seriously, because he had to know she wasn't crazy about their vet. Besides, if he'd been jealous, that would mean he cared. And he'd already said he didn't.

She leaned her head back with a faint sigh, anxious to be home, to get this turbulent evening into the past where it belonged.

But C.C. suddenly pulled off into a small grove of trees, their outline dark against the night sky, and cut off the engine.

She opened her eyes and looked at him. In the pale light from the half moon, his eyes looked glittery and dangerous.

"Afraid?" he asked softly.

"N-no," she faltered.

He put out his cigarette and unfastened first his seat belt, then hers. He took the purse out of her hands and laid it on the dash. With deft sureness, he lifted her body across his legs and eased her head back onto the hard muscle of his upper arm.

"Liar," he said quietly, searching her oval face. "You're scared to death. Physical love isn't something to be afraid of, Pepi. It's an exquisite sharing of all that two people are, an intimate expression of mutual respect and need."

He sounded more gentle than he ever had, and some of her apprehension drained away. She rested her cool hand on his dinner jacket as she searched the hard face above hers. Once she'd dreamed of lying in his arms like this, being totally alone with him and wanted by him. But so much had happened in the meantime that it seemed somehow unreal.

"Do you really want me, that way?" she asked, her voice sounding strained and high-pitched.

"You greenhorn," he murmured. He shifted her so that her belly lay against his, and he rotated her hips sharply, letting her feel what happened to him almost instantly. He heard her gasp and felt her stiffen against him. "Does this answer your question?" he asked outrageously, and his steely hand refused to let her draw away from the stark intimacy. "Would you like to know how many years it's been since a woman could turn me on this fast?"

Her fingers clenched on his dinner jacket, but she stopped trying to pull away. The feel of him was drugging her. Her own body began to betray her, reacting unexpectedly to the evidence of his need and lifting closer to it.

He caught his breath. "Pepi!" he ground out.

She felt him tremble with a sense of wonder. She watched his face and repeated the tiny movement of her hips. Yes, he liked it. She could tell by the way his jaw tautened, by the sudden catch of his breath, the stiffening shudder of his body against her.

"Do you . . . like that?" she whispered shyly.

"Yes, I like it!" he groaned. He bent, his free hand tangling in her thick, soft hair, the other going to the base of her spine to hold her even closer. "Do it again, baby," he whispered against her lips. "Do it again, hard . . . !"

His mouth invaded hers. She felt the sudden sharp thrust of his tongue and her body arched as his hand went under the skirt of her dress and up against her stocking-clad leg. He touched her inner thighs, his mouth teasing now, nibbling at her lips while his hand slowly discovered the most intimate things about her trembling body. She couldn't even protest. She loved what he was doing to her.

His hand withdrew and went up her back to the zipper of the dress, to loosen it before he did the same thing with the catch of her lacy bra.

"Don't be afraid," he said softly when she tried feebly to stay the downward movement of his hands. "I want to look at your breasts, Pepi. I want to touch them."

She trembled all over with the words, her eyes lost in his. She gave way, and the dress fell to her waist along with the thin wisp of lace that had hidden her from his rapt stare.

He held her a little away from him, and his dark eyes feasted on her nudity in the dim light. She could feel the tension in him. He didn't move or speak for the longest time, and as she watched, her nipples began to harden under that piercing stare. She didn't understand the contraction, or the way her body arched up faintly, as if enticing him to do more than look.

"It isn't enough, is it, little one?" he asked tenderly. His hands slid under her bare back and he bent his dark head to her body. "You smell of gardenias, Pepi," he whispered. His lips touched the silken swell of her breast, lightly brushing it, and she shivered. He liked that reaction, so he did it again, and again, working his way around, but not touching the hard nipple. Pepi's hands clenched against his chest and she felt her body beginning to throb in a new and scary way.

"C.C.," she moaned. "Please... it aches so! Make it ... stop!"

One lean hand slid up her rib cage to tease at the outside edge of her breast. His lips teased some more, until she actually shuddered with the need and began to beg him.

"Sweet," he breathed roughly. And his mouth suddenly opened, taking the hard nipple inside, closing on it with a warm, slow suction that made her cry out. It was like a tiny climax. Her hands tangled convulsively in his hair and she wept, gasping as the pleasure went on and on and on.

"Oh, God...!" he ground out, shocked at her capacity for lovemaking. If she could be this aroused when he'd barely touched her, he could hardly imagine how it would be in bed, with her naked body under his, her long, elegant legs enclosing him, holding him, welcoming him as a lover.

"Connal," she whispered shakily. Her lips touched his forehead, his closed eyes, trembling. "Connal, please. Please."

"I can't," he bit off, lifting his head. He could barely speak, his lean hand unsteady on her breast where it rested like a brand of fire while he looked down at his handiwork. "Not here."

"No one would see us," she moaned.

"I can't take the risk," he said heavily. He pulled her to him, wrapping up her bare breasts against the silky fabric of his dinner jacket, rocking her. "Anyone could drive up here, including the county police," he murmured at her ear. His lips brushed her earlobe. "I don't want anyone to see you without your clothes except me. And when we go all the way, I want it to be in a bed, not the front seat of a car."

She shivered, nestling closer. "Does it feel like this, when you go all the way?" she asked huskily.

"Yes," he breathed at her ear. "But it's much more intense." He bit her earlobe and his hands smoothed over her bare back with slow sensuality. "Has Hale seen you like this?" he whispered.

"No," she whispered back. "Nobody has, except you."

He lifted his head and looked down at her, making a meal of her bareness. He touched her nipple, very gently, and watched it harden, felt her shiver. His eyes caught hers. "Much more of this," he said roughly, "and I'll take you sitting up, right here. We'd better go home."

Her body exploded with heat as he lifted her back into her own seat. "Could we do it, like that?" she asked hoarsely.

His face tautened and for one insane instant, he was tempted. "Yes, we could." He banked down the fires. "But we're not going to. We're married. We don't have to make out in cars. Here, sweetheart, let me help you."

He forced himself to control the singeing need in his body as he put her bra and dress back in place, delighted with her headlong response and the certainty that their marriage had a chance after all.

"I don't want to stop," she whispered.

"Neither do I. But we'll wait a while, all the same," he said curtly. He searched her face. "Before we both get blinded and sidetracked by intimacy, I want a little time for us to get to know each other. We'll go see my family and we'll do some things together. Then we'll sleep together."

She was stunned. That had to mean he cared a little, it had to! "I'd like that, Connal," she said.

He smiled at her. "Yes. So would I." He started the car and waited until she fastened her seat belt to drive off. But he held her hand the rest of the way home.

Chapter Ten

Pepi and C.C. left the next morning for Jacobsville. Ben waved them off, muttering something about not knowing how he was going to keep from bursting with all that freedom and being alone with the apple pie Pepi had baked him that morning.

She hadn't been sure what to pack, so she put in her finest clothes and hoped for the best. None of her things were very expensive. She had a feeling that where she was going, they'd look like rags. But she didn't say that to C.C. He was suddenly very distant as he drove.

"You're not having second thoughts, are you?" she asked hesitantly. "About taking me to meet your mother, I mean?"

He glanced at her, astonished. "Why should I?"

She shifted and glanced out at the flat horizon. "Well, C.C., I don't know a lot about fancy place settings and etiquette, and I stayed up half the night worrying about what would happen if I got flustered and spilled coffee on her carpet or something.''

He reached over and found her hand, entwining her cold, nervous fingers with his strong, warm ones.

''Now, listen. My mother is a ranch wife. She's as down-to-earth as your father, and she doesn't have one of those houses that get featured in the designer magazines. If you spilled coffee she'd just point you toward the kitchen and tell you where she keeps the spot remover. Fancy place settings aren't necessary, because Jeanie May cooks such great meals that nobody cares about formal etiquette once they get to the table. The only real hazard is going to be my brother Harden, who'll go off into a black study at the thought of having to help entertain you.''

''Who hurt him like that, made him so bitter?'' she asked.

He glanced at her. ''Well, you'll hear it sooner or later. Better you hear it from me. About a year after Evan was born, my mother and father got a separation. During that time, she met and fell in love with another man. There was a brief affair. Her lover was killed in Vietnam and she came back to my father finally because he kept pleading with her. She was pregnant with Harden, so Dad adopted him. But Jacobsville is a small town, and inevitably, Harden found out the hard way that he wasn't Dad's son.''

''And he blames your mother.''

''That's right, he does. Despite the fact that she's a pillar of the community now, Harden can't forget that she took a lover while she was still legally married. He can't forgive her for making him conspicuous, an outcast as he calls it.''

"But your father adopted him, doesn't that count for anything?" she asked.

He shook his head. "Harden has the most rigid views of any of us. He's an old-line conservative with Neanderthal principles." He glanced toward her with a rueful smile. "I'd bet you that he's still a virgin. I don't think he's even had a woman."

Her eyes widened. She remembered Harden's astonishing good looks, his physique, his rugged personality. Harden a virgin? She burst out laughing. "Not nice," she accused. "Teasing me like that."

"I'm not teasing, as it happens, I'm serious," he replied. "Harden is a deacon in the church and he sings in the choir. In fact, there was a time when he seriously considered being a minister."

"How old is he?"

"Thirty-one."

"A year older than you?" she asked.

He nodded. "Mother and Dad had a rather physical reunion when she came home. They were happy together, but I don't think she ever really got over the other man. And despite the fact that Harden hates her, he's her favorite even now."

"Forgiveness is a virtue," she said. "I guess not everybody is capable of it, but I'm sorry for your mother."

"You won't be, when you meet her. She's spunky. Like you."

She leaned her head back and smiled at him, her eyes faintly possessive. Memories of the night before streamed back to fire her blood and lingered in her pale brown eyes.

He stopped at an intersection and looked back at her, his own eyes kindling with what he read in that level stare.

"Remembering?" he asked huskily.

"Yes," she whispered.

His breath came more quickly, his brown sports shirt rising and falling roughly over his broad chest. His gaze went down to her breasts under the pale green shirtwaist dress she was wearing and lingered there. "You were like warm silk under my mouth," he bit off.

She gasped.

His eyes lifted back to hers and time stopped. "This isn't the place," he said tightly.

"No."

He glanced around and behind them. Not a single car in sight. "On the other hand, what the hell," he murmured and threw the car out of gear. "Come here."

He snapped open her seat belt and pulled her to him, his hard mouth crushing down over hers in a fever of ardent need. She circled his head with her arms and held on for dear life, giving him back the kiss hungrily. Her body throbbed with need of him, her mouth shaking as his tongue penetrated it insistently.

He dragged his head up at the distant sound of a big truck coming closer and spotted it in the rearview mirror. "Obviously he's not a married man," he muttered, putting a radiant, breathless Pepi back in her seat and buckling her in. "Damn it." He put the car in gear again, his hands slightly unsteady on the wheel, looked both ways and pulled out onto the highway.

He glanced at her hungrily. "Tonight, I'm going to have you. One way or the other, the waiting's over."

Her lips parted on a rough breath. "Are the walls very thin?" she asked hesitantly.

"We'll be in a room away from the others," he said curtly. "You can scream if you want to, nobody will hear you."

"I . . . I can't seem to be quiet when you start touching me," she said gently. "I lose control."

"So do I," he replied tersely.

She flushed. He made it sound very intimate and she wanted him. Her body blazed with the need, even now.

He glanced at her. "Baby, if you don't stop looking at me like that, I'll park the damned car and make love to you on the roadside," he threatened huskily.

"Anywhere," she said shakily. "Oh, Connal, I want you so much, it's like a fever."

His jaw tautened. He actually shivered. His eyes went to a small crossroads where a motel was situated. Without thinking, he pulled off and cut the engine. "Do you want me enough?" he asked, staring at her.

The fever was so high that even her shyness didn't faze it. "Yes," she whispered huskily, flushing.

He got out, went inside the office and came out with a key. He didn't say another word until they were in the room, with the door locked.

"Do you want me to use anything?" he asked before he touched her.

She knew what he was asking. She loved him. If a child came of this, it would be all right. He wanted one desperately, she knew.

"No," she said, going close to him. "Don't use anything."

He drew her slowly to him, already so aroused that his tall, fit body was shaking. "I don't know how long I can hold out," he breathed at her lips. "But I'll try to arouse you enough to make it bearable. And later, afterward, I'll make it up to you if I lose control."

She didn't understand what he was saying. His hands were on the buttons of her dress and she stood very still, letting him peel the clothing from her body until she was totally nude.

Her skin felt blazing hot. She was shy, and the way he was looking at her burned her, but it made her proud, too, because his pleasure in her body was evident in the glitter of his black eyes and the tenderness of his smile.

He jerked back the covers on the big double bed and picked her up, putting her down gently against the pillows. Then he set about removing his own clothing.

Pepi had seen pictures of naked men, but nothing had prepared her for the sight of Connal without clothing. He was magnificent, all lean hard muscle and black, curling hair. Aroused, his body was faintly intimidating and she held her breath when he came toward her.

"Don't panic," he said gently as he slid onto the bed beside her. "By the time we start, you'll be ready for me. Your body is like a pink rosebud, all silky and tightly furled. I'm going to open the petals, one by one, and make you bloom for me." He bent his mouth and took hers, very softly. One lean hand slid down her rib cage to her hips and over her thighs and back up to tease around her breast.

The embarrassment and shyness faded as he began to touch her, his fingers delicate and deft and sure on her untaught body. He lifted his head and looked at her, watched her reactions as he feathered caresses over her taut breasts, down her flat belly, to that place where she was most a woman. He touched her there and she shivered and tried to get away.

"No," he whispered tenderly, kissing her eyes closed. "This is part of it. You have to give yourself completely, or I could hurt you even without meaning to. I want to show you how it's going to feel. Relax, little one. Give me your body."

His lips coaxed lazily, and she gave in to the slow, tender probing of his fingers, shivering as she permitted the extraordinary intimacy. Her body reacted to him with headlong delight, arching and throbbing as he made it feel incredible sensations with his deft touch.

"It won't even be difficult for you," he whispered, smiling against her mouth. "Now it begins, little one. Now..."

The kiss grew deeper, invasive. His hand tormented and then began to move with a slow, torturously sweet rhythm that made her lift and tremble with each touch. She gasped and then little cries began to purr out of her. She reached for him, her nails digging into his upper arms as the pleasure built beyond anything she'd ever dreamed.

He smiled through his own fierce pleasure at the look on her face. His head bent to her breasts and he took one into his mouth with the same rhythmic movement his fingers were teaching her. All at once, she began to convulse.

And at that moment, he lifted his body completely over hers, nudging her long, shivering legs aside, and thrust down with one fierce, smooth movement.

She cried out, her eyes meeting his at the instant he took possession of her. But she didn't draw back, even at the faintly piercing pain that quickly diminished in the face of a slow, anguished pleasure that fed on itself and grew and grew with each sharp, downward movement of his body.

Somewhere along the way, his taut face became a blur, and she shuddered into oblivion just as she heard his hoarse cry and felt the deep, dragging convulsions of his body.

She opened her eyes at last, feeling new, reborn. Her skin was damp and cool. So was his. He was lying over her, dead weight now that the passion had drained out of him, and her arms enfolded him tenderly, holding him to her. She moved and felt him move with her, awed by the fusion of her female body with his male one, with the devastating intimacy of lovemaking.

"Did it hurt very much?" he asked at her ear, his voice drowsy with pleasure.

"No." Her arms contracted. "Do it again."

He chuckled. "I need a few minutes," he whispered. "Men aren't blessed with the capacity of women."

"Really?" She looked into his eyes as he lifted his dark, sweaty head. "You cried out."

"So did you," he said lazily. "Or don't you remember?"

"It all sort of blurred at the last," she replied. Her eyes mirrored her awe. "I hope I get a baby," she whispered. "It was so beautiful."

His face tautened and to his astonishment he felt his body react to the words with sudden, sharp capability.

She gasped. "Connal! You said—"

"Never mind what I said," he bit off against her mouth. His arms caught his weight and he began to move hungrily. "Help me this time," he whispered, and taught her how. "Yes, like that, like . . . that," he gasped, shivering as the wave began to catch him all over again. Impossible, he thought while he could. His teeth clenched. He could feel her eyes on him. She was . . . watching him . . . and he was so caught up in the fevered need that he didn't even mind. Her body, soft like down, silky, hot, absorbed him into it, holding him . . .

He arched, hoping against hope that she was still with him as he felt the sensation blind him with pleasure.

"Are you all right?"

He heard her voice and managed to open his eyes. She was above him, now, her face concerned, her pale brown eyes curious and gentle.

His heart was still slamming wildly against his chest. He could barely breathe. He pushed back his damp hair and drew her mouth down to his, kissing her tenderly.

"Yes, I'm all right," he whispered.

"You looked scary," she managed. "Like you were being killed. And you cried out..."

He laughed wearily. "My God, honey, why do you think the French call it the little death?" he asked. He drew her hand to his mouth. "You look the same way," he added, smiling. "I watched you, the first time."

"Oh." She colored a little. "I watched you, the second."

"Yes, I know." Hid dark eyes held hers. "It's all right," he said when she looked faintly guilty. "Total intimacy is a gift, something that two people share. Don't be embarrassed by anything you say or do when you're with me like this. I'll never ridicule you with it. I want you to feel completely uninhibited when we make love, as free to take me as I am to take you."

Her eyes widened. "Could I?"

"Well, not right now," he murmured ruefully.

"I didn't mean right now. You'd let me?"

He frowned slightly. "Of course I'd let you. You're my wife."

"And you...won't mind if I get pregnant right away?" she persisted.

"I told you I wanted a child," he said simply. His dark eyes narrowed. "They say a woman can tell at the instant of conception," he murmured.

She smiled down at him gently. "I don't think I can," she said. The smile faded and she traced his thin lips with a trembling forefinger. "Connal, what if I can't give you a child?" she asked worriedly. "Will you want a divorce...?"

"No!" He dragged her down to him and kissed her roughly. His eyes blazed at her. "It isn't a conditional marriage," he said firmly. "If you can't, it won't matter, so stop thinking up things to worry about."

"All right." She relaxed against him, sighing with pleasure as she felt the crisp hair on his broad chest tickling her breasts. She laughed softly and moved deliberately from side to side. "That feels good," she whispered.

"Yes, indeed, it does," he murmured, indulging her. "But you've had enough for one day. You're much too new to the art for long sessions in bed."

She opened her eyes and stared across his hair-covered chest to the window beyond. "Connal, it's addictive, isn't it?" she asked lazily. "Once you know what it's like, you want it more every time."

"Yes." His arms contracted. "No regrets?"

"Not even one," she whispered. She closed her eyes and nestled closer, smoothing one of her long legs against his powerful, hair-roughened one. "I ache."

"So do I," he confessed. "But we have to stop."

She sat up, her eyes slow and possessive on his body, openly curious. He watched her with evident amusement as she learned him by sight.

"I've never seen a man without his clothes before," she said.

"I'm glad. You won't be able to compare me unfavorably with anyone else," he mused.

She laughed. "As if anybody could compare with you," she murmured. "You're beautiful, Connal. You're just beautiful."

He sat up and kissed her warmly. "Men aren't beautiful," he said firmly, and got up to dress.

"Handsome, then. Physically devastating." She stretched hugely, enjoying the way his eyes slid over her appreciatively. "I used to think about being with you, like this, but it was always night and the lights were out."

"What a shock you were in for," he said dryly.

She stood up, smiling at him. "It was a very nice shock, actually," she said.

He pulled her gently into his arms and kissed her. "I hope I gave you half as much pleasure as you gave me," he whispered. "The fact that you came to me a virgin is something I'll treasure all my life."

She hugged him fiercely. "You make me glad that I waited," she murmured. "None of my friends did. They used to make fun of me."

"I never will," he said, tapping her gently on the nose. His eyes were brilliant with some inner feeling. "Get your clothes on."

"Fancy telling a woman that," she sighed. "And after she's given you everything she has."

"Oh, I'd keep you like that forever," he murmured, tracing her soft lines with his eyes. "But people are bound to stare if you go out like that."

"I get your point." She put her clothes on again and brushed her hair. Connal was waiting when she came out of the bathroom.

"Is this dress all right?" she asked worriedly. "I won't look too out of place, will I?"

He tilted her face up and kissed her. "You look just right, Mrs. Tremayne."

"I like the way that sounds," she whispered, thinking that it would be even more special if he loved her as much as she loved him. But he'd been gentle, and he must care for her a little to have been so tender.

"Legally mine," he murmured. His eyes darkened. "So don't give Evan any ideas."

Her face mirrored her shock. "I've only seen him once," she began.

"He thinks you're the berries," he replied. "And he's a lonely man. Don't encourage him."

"I noticed you didn't mention Harden. Don't you want to protect him, too?"

He ignored the sarcasm, shocked by his own possessiveness, his sudden sharp jealousy. "Harden's immune. Evan isn't."

"Listen here, C. C. Tremayne, just because I liked sleeping with you is no reason to accuse me of being a loose woman...!"

"Point one," he said, covering her lips with a firm forefinger, "I am not accusing you of anything. And point two, what we just did together had nothing, not a damned thing, to do with sleeping."

"Ticky, ticky," she returned.

He searched her eyes slowly. "I've never had it like that," he said curtly. "Not with anyone. Not so bad that I cried out and damned near fainted from the force of the pleasure when you satisfied me. I don't know that I like losing control that savagely."

She felt a fierce pride that she'd done that to him, and her eyes told him so. "Suppose I make you like it?" she whispered huskily.

His heart began to thunder against his ribs all over again at her sultry tone. "Think you could?" he challenged.

She moved closer, her finger toying with one of the pearly buttons at his throat. "Wait and see," she said softly. She reached up and teased his lips with hers, a fleeting touch that aroused without satisfying.

He watched her go to the door with a feeling of having given up a part of himself that he was going to miss like hell one day. She knew how he reacted to her, and that gave her a weapon. She enjoyed lovemaking, that was obvious, but she'd said she didn't love him. If she ever realized how hopelessly in love with her he was, she'd have him on the end of a hook that he'd never get free from. He almost shivered with apprehension. Accidental marriage or not, he wanted this woman with blind obsession. Whatever happened now, he wasn't going to give her up.

They drove the rest of the way to Jacobsville in a tense silence. C.C. smoked cigarettes until Pepi had to let down a window in self-defense. He seemed nervous, and she wondered if it was coming home that had him in such a state, or bringing her here. Despite his denials, she wondered how she was going to be received by his family. He was used to wealth and society people, and she wasn't. Would they even accept her?

He drove past a huge feedlot, through the country and down a long winding paved road until he reached an arch that boasted a sign that read Tremayne.

"Home," he murmured, smiling at her. He sped down the driveway in the Ford, while Pepi clenched her hands in her lap and hoped that she could cope. There were white fences on either side of the driveway, and far in the distance sat a white Victorian house with a long porch and beautiful gingerbread latticework. There were flower beds everywhere, and right now assorted chrysanthemums were blooming in them.

"It's beautiful," she said, her eyes lingering on the tall trees around the house.

"I've always thought so. There's Mother."

Theodora Tremayne was small and thin and dark, with silver hair that gleamed in the sun. She was wearing jeans and a sweatshirt with an apron. She rushed out to meet them.

"Thank God you're home," she said, hugging Connal. "You must be Pepi, I'm so glad to meet you." She hugged Pepi, too, before she turned back to her tall son. "The sink in the kitchen is stopped up and I can't find Evan anywhere! Can you fix it?"

"Don't you have a plumber's helper?" Connal asked with a wry smile.

"Of course. What do you want with it?" she asked blankly.

"She had a flat tire on the wheelbarrow," he told Pepi.

"Go ahead, blurt out all the shameful family secrets at once!" Theodora raged at him. "Why don't you tell her about the mouse under the sink that I can't catch, and the snake who insists on living in my root cellar?"

Pepi burst out laughing. She couldn't help it. She'd been so afraid of some rich society matron who'd make fun of her, and here instead was Theodora Tremayne, who was nothing short of a leprechaun.

"I'm glad to see you have a sense of humor, Pepi," Theodora said approvingly. "You'll need it if you have to live with my son. He has no sense of humor. None of my sons do. They all walk around like thunderheads, glowering at everybody."

"Nobody glowers except Harden," C.C. said defensively.

"He's enough," Theodora said miserably. "He gets worse all the time. Well, come in and fix the sink, son. Pepi, do you like ham sandwiches? I'm afraid that's all I could get together in a hurry. I've been out helping Evan and the boys brand new calves and things are in a bit of a mess.''

She went on mumbling ahead of them. Connal caught Pepi's hand.

"No more worried thoughts?" he asked with an amused smile.

"None at all. She's a treasure!" she said.

He slid his arm around her and hugged her close. "She isn't the only treasure around here," he whispered, and bent to kiss her.

Pepi went inside with him, her feet barely touching the floor. She wondered if she wouldn't float right up to the ceiling, she was so happy. He had to care a little. He just had to!

Chapter Eleven

But Connal's earlier warmth seemed to disintegrate as the day wore on. He fixed his mother's sink, leaving Pepi to help a flustered Theodora set the dining-room table.

"I'm so glad he's coming out of the past," Theodora told the younger woman with sincere gratitude. "You don't know how it's been for us, watching him beat himself to death over something he couldn't have helped. He came to see us, occasionally, and there were phone calls and letters. But it's not the same thing as regular contact."

"We never knew anything about his past; Dad and I, that is," Pepi said. "But C.C. always had class. You couldn't miss it. I used to wonder why he buried himself on a run-down place like ours."

"He speaks highly of your father," Theodora said. "And he, uh, had a lot to say about you, too, the last time he was here."

Pepi blushed, lowering her eyes to the plate she was putting on the table. Thank God she knew where the knife, fork and spoon went, and it wasn't one of those elaborate settings that she couldn't figure out. "I guess he did," she answered Theodora. "He was furious when he left the ranch. I didn't blame him, you know," she said, lifting quiet brown eyes to the other woman's face. "He had every right to hate me for not telling him the truth."

Theodora searched those soft eyes. "He's hurt you badly, hasn't he?" she asked unexpectedly. "Does he know how you feel?"

The blush got worse. Pepi's hand shook as she laid the silverware. "No," she said in a whisper. "If he even considers it, he probably thinks I'm in the throes of physical attraction. And for right now, it's safer that way. I'm not convinced that I can ever be the kind of wife he needs. You see," she added worriedly, "I'm not sophisticated."

Theodora impulsively went around the table and hugged her, warmly. "If he lets you get away from him, I'll beat him with a big stick," she said forcefully. "I'll go and bring in the sandwiches and call the boys in. Don't look so worried, Penelope, they won't take any bites out of you!" she said with a grin.

Pepi sat down where Theodora had indicated, and a minute or so later, the older woman came back with a huge platter of sandwiches, closely followed by her three towering sons.

"Hello, again," Evan said warmly, seating himself beside Pepi. "What a treat, having something pretty to look at while I eat," he added, with a meaningful glance toward his brother Harden.

Harden lifted a dark eyebrow, glancing with cold in-difference at Pepi. "I've told you before, if you don't like looking at me while you eat, wear a blindfold."

"God forbid, he'd probably eat the tablecloth!" Theodora chuckled. "Sit down, Connal, don't dither."

"Yes, ma'am," he murmured, but his smile wasn't re-flected in his eyes as he glanced with open disapproval at Evan sitting beside Pepi.

"Say Grace, Harden," Theodora said.

He did, and everyone became occupied with sand-wiches and coffee preparation. Evan told Pepi about the ranch and its history while Harden ate in silence and Theodora quizzed Connal about his future plans.

Pepi couldn't hear what Connal was saying, but she did feel the angry lash of his eyes. She wondered what she'd done to make him so cold toward her. Could he be re-gretting that impulsive stop at the motel? She flushed a little, embarrassed at the memories that flooded her mind. She still ached pleasantly from the experience. But perhaps it was different for a man, if he didn't love a woman he slept with. Connal had wanted her with a rag-ing passion, she couldn't have mistaken that. But after-ward he might have regretted his loss of control, the lapse that had turned an accidental marriage into a real one. He might be having second thoughts about Edie even now. He looked odd, too. Very taciturn and quiet. Pepi knew that mood very well. It was the one that caused the men to keep well away from him, because when he got broody, he got quick-tempered, too. Pepi hoped he wasn't spoiling for a fight with her.

"I always wanted a sister," Evan murmured dryly. "What I got was Connal and Donald and . . . him," he shuddered as he glanced at Harden.

Harden kept eating, totally impervious to the insult.

"You won't get through his hide with insults," Theodora told her son. "I tend to think he thrives on them."

"You should know," Harden told her, his blue eyes as cold as the smile he bent on her.

"Not now," she told him firmly. "We have guests."

"Family," Evan corrected.

"Yours, not mine," Harden said with a pointed glare at his mother. "No offense," he added to Connal.

"You plan to carry the vendetta to your grave, I gather," Theodora muttered.

"I've got to get back to work," Harden said, rising. "I'll see you tonight, Connal."

He walked out, lean and lithe and arrow-straight, without a backward glance.

"Now that the company has improved, what do you think of our quaint little place?" Evan asked Pepi.

She replied automatically, her mind on the awkward conversation that had gone before. If this was any indication of how things were going to go for the duration of her visit, she wasn't at all sure she wanted to stay.

But it got better, without Harden's difficult presence. Evan took her in hand before Connal could protest and drove off with her in the ranch Jeep.

"What about Connal . . . ?" she asked uneasily, glancing back to where he stood with Theodora glaring after them.

"Now, now, all I have in mind is a little brotherly chat," Evan replied, and the teasing was abruptly gone. As he glanced at her without smiling, she saw in Evan the same steely character that had intimidated her first in C.C. and then in Harden.

He pulled the Jeep off on the side of the ranch road when they were out of sight of the house, and cut the engine. "Edie called here this morning, looking for Connal," he said without preamble.

"Oh. I see." She studied the broad, leonine features quietly. He and Connal looked alike. Although Evan's hair was more brown than black, he had the same piercing, unsmiling sternness as his brother.

"I don't think you do," Evan replied. "Edie isn't the kind of woman to take a rebuff lying down. She didn't believe him when he told her he was married. She thought he was being tricked by a fake license, and she told me so."

She sighed heavily. "Well, it's easy enough to check, you know," she said.

"Undoubtedly. I did, when Connal showed us the license." He smiled ruefully at her glare. "No offense, child, but he stands to inherit a hell of a fortune when Mother passes on. He's not exactly a poverty case now, and I didn't know you from a peanut when he came storming in here waving that damned license and cursing at the top of his lungs."

"But Connal said it was you who changed his mind about staying married to me," she faltered.

He leaned back against the Jeep door, big and elegant-looking for a cattleman, his Stetson pushed back over his broad forehead. "Sure I did," he mused. "One of these days I'll let you read what my private detective said about you. You're the kind of woman mothers dream about finding for their sons. A walking, talking little elf with domestic skills and a gentle heart. In this oversexed, undercompassionate generation, you're a miracle. I told Connal so. Eventually he began to realize that he could do a lot worse."

"I wonder." She sighed.

"Edie doesn't seem to agree, so watch out," he cautioned sternly. "Don't let her spring any surprises on you. Forewarned is forearmed, right?"

"Right. Thanks, Evan."

"Connal deserves a little happiness," he said tersely. "He never had much with Marsha, and she couldn't bear to have him out of her sight five seconds. It's time he stopped beating himself to death."

"I think so, too," she said gently. "I'll take good care of him, Evan." *If I get to,* she added silently.

He smiled almost tenderly. "I gather that you've been doing that very well for the past three years," he said, his deep voice warm with affection. "We'd better get back. I thought you ought to know what the competition was up to so there wouldn't be any unexpected surprises."

"I'll watch my back," she promised.

Evan drove her around the ranch and pointed out herd sires along the way. He seemed to have a phenomenal memory for their names, because he never seemed to draw a blank. He was in a jovial mood for the rest of the way home.

But Connal was in a furious one when they got there. He gave his brother a glare that would have fried a defenseless egg, and the one he bent on Pepi made her feel like backing away.

Theodora pretended not to notice the tension. She herded them into her four-by-four and they drove into Jacobsville to get some more supplies for roundup.

She seemed to know everyone. Pepi lost her nervousness as she was introduced to several people at the hardware store, including a harassed young woman herding three small children through the aisles, followed by a tall blond man.

"The Ballengers," Theodora told Pepi, "Abby and Calhoun. That's Matt…no, it's Terry…and that's Edd," she said, trying to identify each child.

"You've got it just backward, Theodora," Calhoun drawled. "Terry, Edd and Matt."

"Between your kids and your brother Justin's children, I can't keep the names straight!"

"And Justin and Shelby have another one on the way," Calhoun chuckled. "Shelby's sure this one is going to be a girl."

"After two boys I can understand her determination," Theodora replied.

"We gave up," Abby sighed. "I like boys and I'm tired of the maternity ward, not to mention never being able to get one word in edgewise. They'd trample my dead body to get to their Daddy."

"They sure would, but I still love you," Calhoun murmured and kissed her forehead warmly.

She melted against him, almost visibly a part of him. Pepi felt a twinge of sadness that she might never know that kind of devotion. Apparently desire was all she aroused in C.C., and the way he was acting, he might not even feel that anymore. His lean face was as hard as if it had been carved out of granite, and he didn't move a step closer to Pepi when she was introduced as his wife. It was hard to pretend that everything was fine, that she was divinely happy, when her heart was breaking.

Later, Theodora took her on a tour of Jacobsville, named after Shelby Ballenger's family, and pointed out the huge Ballenger feedlot and the old Jacobs's home, now owned by a new resident. Back at the ranch, Theodora produced photo albums, while the men went out to check on the progress of the branding.

There was little conversation over the supper table. The pert, gangly cook made some acid comments about the enormous male appetites and grinned on her way back to the kitchen.

"She's been here for so long that she owns the kitchen," Theodora explained merrily. "She loves clean platters after a meal."

"She's a wonderful cook," Pepi mused.

"I hear you make wonderful apple pies," Evan commented dryly.

"I don't know about that," Pepi said shyly. "My dad seems to think they're pretty good, because he sure hates sharing them."

"I don't blame him." Evan glared at Harden and his mother. "I hardly ever get my fair share of any dessert around here."

Theodora's eyebrows arched. "Penelope, his idea of a fair share is two-thirds of the pie."

"I'm going seedy, anybody can see that," Evan protested. "Wasting away from starvation..."

Pepi laughed delightedly, her eyes twinkling at Evan, who was sitting beside her.

Across the table, Connal wasn't laughing. He was tormenting himself with that smile and reading all sorts of ridiculous ideas into it. She'd been attracted to Evan since the first time she'd seen him, and today she'd gone off with him all too willingly. Now she was hanging on his every word. He was losing Pepi. If all she'd felt for him was a sensual curiosity, now that he'd satisfied that, she might have no interest left in him. God, what if she fell in love with Evan? His face contorted and he averted it quickly, before anyone saw his anguish.

After supper, Theodora produced a new video as a special treat, a first-run comedy that Pepi had been dying to see. But her enthusiasm quickly waned when C.C. left in the middle stating that he needed to make a few business calls.

Pepi excused herself shortly thereafter and went toward the study, hoping to have it out with C.C. But he wasn't there. With a leaden sigh, she went out the front door, pulling her sweater closer around her, and sat alone on the steps to look out over the dark horizon.

The door opened and closed. Expecting, hoping, that it was C.C., she got to her feet. But it was Harden.

Of all the men she'd ever met, he made her the most nervous.

"Am I intruding?" he asked quietly.

"No. I...just wanted a little air," she stammered. "I'd better go back in now."

He caught her arm, very gently, and held her in place. "There's no need to be afraid of me," he said softly. "None of my vendettas, as Theodora calls them, involve you."

She relaxed a little when he let her go and lit a cigarette.

"Connal's been watching you all night," he said after a minute. "Brooding. Did you argue before you came here?"

"No," she said, glad of the dark because she blushed remembering what they'd done before they came here. "We were getting along better than we had in some time, in fact. Then when we got here, he closed up."

"About the time you went off with Evan," he suggested.

"Well...yes."

"I thought so."

"But that was so Evan could tell me about the phone call," she said, puzzled.

He moved into the light from the windows, frowning. "What phone call?"

"There's this lady C.C. used to go around with," she said wearily. "Edie. Evan says she called here looking for C.C. because she thinks I faked the marriage license."

"Sour grapes, I expect," he mused. "Did you tell Connal why you went off with Evan?"

"I haven't had a chance. He seems to be avoiding me. I guessed maybe he was having second thoughts, again. He was sure mad when he found out the marriage was valid," she said, grimacing. "I thought he'd never speak to me again as long as he lived. Then when I agreed to an annulment and started the wheels turning, he showed up again and said he didn't want one." She threw up her hands. "I don't know what he wants anymore. Maybe he's missing Edie and angry because he's stuck with me."

"Maybe he's jealous," he murmured dryly. "I see that thought hadn't occurred to you," he added when she gaped at him.

"C.C.'s never been jealous of me," she faltered. "My gosh, he never wanted me. Well, not for a wife, I mean..." She averted her red face when she remembered who she was talking to.

Harden actually laughed, the sound deep and pleasant in the night air. "He's a man. And it does rather go with marriage."

"I suppose so," she murmured. "But he doesn't have any reason to be jealous of Evan. I always wanted a big brother, you see."

"And Evan is a teddy bear, right?"

"Well, yes..."

"That particular teddy bear has some nasty fangs and a temper you're better off not knowing about," he advised. "He likes you, but Marsha wouldn't come near the place because of him. He hated her from head to heels and made no secret of it."

"But he's so nice," she said.

"You're not doing business with him," he chuckled. "Evan's deep. Just don't put too much stock in that boyish charm. I'd hate to have you totally disillusioned when he throws somebody over a fence."

"Evan?" she gasped.

"One of the new men took a short quirt to a filly and drew blood. Evan heaved him over the fence and jumped it himself. The last we saw of the man, he was tearing through the blackberry thicket like a scalded dog trying to outrun Evan."

She was beginning to get a good idea of what the Tremayne men were really like. She whistled silently. "My, my, and here I thought you were the terror of the outfit." She grinned.

"Oh, I'm right down the line behind your husband and Evan."

"And Donald, is that his name, the youngest?"

"Donald puts Tabasco Sauce on his biscuits," he replied. "And I have personally seen him skin men at five feet when he's angry."

"I don't know that I want to be related to you savages," she said, tongue in cheek.

"Sure you do," he replied. "Once you get to know us, you'll feel right at home. Any woman who'll take on Connal has to be a hell-raiser in her own right. God knows Jo Ann is, or she'd never have lasted three years with Donald."

She laughed. "I can't wait to meet them."

"They're away for two weeks on business, I'm sorry to say. Another time."

"Yes." She glanced toward the front door. "I suppose I'd better go and try to find my husband."

"That's a step in the right direction. Good night, Penelope."

"Good night, Harden," she replied, smiling as he went down the steps and out to his car. He was nice. Like the rest of C.C.'s family.

She said good night to the others and went upstairs, wondering if she could work up enough nerve to seduce her own husband.

Chapter Twelve

It was barely ten o'clock, but when Penelope got to the room where Connal had taken their suitcases, it was to find him already in bed and apparently asleep.

She hesitated. The lamp by the king-size bed was on, but the bare chest half-covered by the plaid sheet was rising and falling regularly.

"Connal?" she asked softly, but he didn't answer.

With a long sigh, she got out her gown and took it into the bathroom to put it on. This was not the night she'd envisioned, and her courage failed her when she walked back into the bedroom minutes later wearing the long green nylon gown.

She climbed slowly into bed beside him, gave his dark head and his hair-covered muscular chest a long look, and resignedly turned out the light.

But she couldn't sleep. She tossed and turned, remembering so vividly the ardor she'd shared with C.C. only hours before. Her body had never ached so when she'd been unawakened. Now she knew what desire was, and she felt it so acutely that it was almost pain.

"Can't you sleep?" he asked, his voice deep and clear, not muffled with drowsiness.

"Not very well," she said. She lay on her side, looking toward the dark shape that was his head. Dim light from the safety lights by the barn shone in through the curtains. "I guess it's because I'm not used to sleeping with anyone," she added.

"Neither am I, just lately." He reached out and drew her slowly against him. Her hand came in contact with his bare hip and she realized belatedly that he wasn't wearing pajamas.

He felt her stiffen unexpectedly and chuckled under his breath. "You saw me nude just this morning," he reminded her. "And I saw you. Is it still such a shock? Or is it just that I'm the wrong man?" he added sarcastically.

"The wrong man?" she echoed.

"You've been hanging on Evan all day," he said. His hands smoothed up her body, his thumbs edging out to rub against her sensitive nipples. "Are your marriage vows uncomfortable all of a sudden?"

"C.C., that's not true," she said quietly. "I like Evan very much, but I haven't been hanging on him."

His fingers bit into her sides. "I wouldn't really expect you to admit it. Maybe I can't even blame you. One way or another, I got us into this mess."

A mess. He was admitting that it was that, in his eyes. Her heart plummeted. "I thought you were making a phone call. I went looking for you," she said, making a clean breast of it.

"I made it up here," he said. "I had to call Edie."

Her heart stopped beating. She wanted to hit him. So Evan's warning had been right on the money, had it? That woman wasn't going to give up, and if C.C. had no qualms about calling her from his family home, then he must have misgivings about breaking off with her in the first place.

Connal felt her go rigid and his heart jumped. That was the first hopeful sign he'd ever had that she might care a little for him. God, if only it were true!

"Nothing to say?" he chided.

She ground her teeth together. "I think I can sleep now," she said through them.

"Can you?" He moved the covers away and while she was dealing with that unexpected action, his lips came down squarely over her breast, taking the nipple and the fabric that covered it into the hot darkness of his open mouth.

The cry that tore out of her throat was music to his ears. He shifted and while his mouth made intimate love to hers, he stripped the gown down her trembling body and his hands relearned its soft, sweet contours with a lazy thoroughness that had her moaning in his arms.

"Can I have you without hurting you?" he whispered at her ear, his breath as hot as the body threatening hers.

"Yes," she whimpered. Her nails bit into his shoulders, tugging at them, her legs already parting to admit him, her body lifting to meet the fierce, heated descent of his. "Connal...!"

"Take me," he ground out against her mouth as his hips thrust down in one long, invasive movement.

She whimpered under the sharp pleasure, clinging to him as his body enforced its possession with increasing urgency. "Don't stop, Connal, don't...stop...!"

His mouth bit at hers. "You're noisy," he breathed huskily. "I like it. I like the way you feel, the way you taste. Tell me you want me."

"I...want...you!" She could barely get the words out. He was killing her. The pleasure was too sweet to bear and she was going to die of it.

She said so, her voice breaking as he fulfilled her with savage urgency, finding his own shuddering release seconds later.

She couldn't stop trembling. She clung to his damp body, frightened by the force of the satisfaction he'd given her.

He felt tears against his cheek and lifted his head. His heartbeat was still shaking him, his arms trembling as they supported him above her. He couldn't see her face, but he could feel the convulsive shudders of her body, feel how disturbed she was from the grip of her hands.

"Don't be afraid," he whispered. "We went very high this time. Give yourself time to come down again. It's all right." His fingers smoothed back her damp hair and he kissed her eyes closed, kissed her cheeks, her trembling mouth in a warm, soft silence that gradually took the fear away.

"You said . . . I was noisy," she whispered.

"Didn't I say that I liked it?" he murmured. He bit her lower lip gently. "Touch me."

He guided her hand to him, and smiled when she hesitated shyly.

"We're married," he said. He opened her fingers and spread them, pressing them slowly against him. "You won't hurt me, if that's why you're so tense," he whispered. He kissed her gently and in between kisses, he guided and coaxed and in soft whispers, explained to her everything she needed to know about a man's body.

The lesson was sweet and lazy and slow, and as her eyelids began to fall drowsily, he joined her body tenderly, intimately, to his and pulled her over him to cradle her softness on his strength. Incredibly, she slept.

They went home the next day. Connal was less rigid, and seemed perfectly happy all the way back to the ranch. But he was preoccupied again by the end of the day, and he didn't mention sharing her bed that night.

It became a routine for several days. He was friendly enough, even affectionate, but he didn't touch her or kiss her. He did watch her, with brooding, narrow eyes as if he couldn't decide what to do.

She was still worried about the phone call he said he'd made to Edie, and if his desire for her had waned because of the other woman.

"What's going on between you and my new son-in-law?" Ben Mathews finally demanded one morning in the kitchen after breakfast.

"What do you mean?" she hedged. She had her hair in a ponytail and she was wearing a sweater and jeans and scuffs, less than elegant attire. C.C. hadn't even come in for breakfast for the second time in as many days.

"I mean, you and Connal are married, but you don't act like it," he said bluntly. "And ever since you came home from his family's ranch, you've both gone broody. Why?"

"He called Edie," she said quietly. "I don't know if he's looking for a way out or trying to make me get a divorce. He hasn't said. But he's not happy, I know that." She glanced at him, hoping to forestall any more personal questions. "Don't you have to be in El Paso at eleven for a meeting?" she asked.

"Yes, I do, and I'm going any minute. Why not an annulment?"

She blushed and put her hands back in the warm, soapy dishwater. "For the obvious reason," she said demurely.

"Then if that's the case, why aren't you living together? There's a furnished house going spare, if that's the problem."

She felt tears stinging her eyes. "It's more than that."

"What?"

She dropped a pan and in the ensuing noise, nobody heard C.C. come in the front door and down the hall. He was standing right outside the door, about to make his presence known, when he heard Pepi's choked voice.

"I'll tell you what," she wept. "He doesn't love me. He never did, and I didn't expect it, you know. But I had hoped..."

Ben pulled her gently into his arms and held her while she cried. "You poor kid," he sighed, patting her back comfortingly. "I don't guess you ever told him you were dying for love of him?"

Connal felt his body go rigid with the shock. He couldn't have moved if his life had depended on it.

"No, I never told him," Pepi sobbed. "Three years. Three long, awful years. And we got married by accident, and I knew he wouldn't want somebody plain and tomboyish like me, but oh, God, Papa, I love him so much! What am I going to do?"

Connal moved into the room, white-faced, his dark eyes blazing. "You might try telling him," he said harshly.

Ben let her go and moved away, a smug grin on his face that he quickly hid from them. "I'm late. Better be off. See you kids after lunch."

They didn't even hear him leave. Connal was still staring at her with an expression she could barely see through her tears.

"Oh, mother!" she wailed. "Why did you have to stand out there and listen!"

"Why not?" He moved closer, catching her arms and jerking her close, his bat-wing chaps hard and cold even through her jeans, like the tan checked Western shirt her hands rested against. "Say it to my face. Tell me you love me," he dared, his taut expression a challenge in itself, giving nothing away of his own feelings.

"All right. I love you!" she burst out. "There, are you satisfied?" she raged, red-faced.

"Not yet," he murmured in a low, sexy tone. "But I think I can take care of that little problem right here..."

His mouth settled on hers in slow, arousing movements. It had been so long. Days of polite conversation, tormented lonely nights aching for what had been. She went wild in his arms, pressing close against him, welcoming the intimate touch of his hands on her breasts, their pressure at her thighs as he moved her urgently against his hips.

"Just a minute," he whispered gruffly, as he locked the door.

His hand then went to the chaps. He stripped them off and threw them on the floor, his hands going to her blouse and then her jeans. Somehow he managed to get them off along with the scuffs she'd been wearing instead of boots. He sat down in the chair at the kitchen table and pulled her over him.

There was a metallic sound as his belt hit the floor and the rasp of a zipper. He pulled her down on him, watching her eyes as she absorbed him easily, quickly.

"Forgive me," he whispered jerkily. "I can't wait."

"Neither can I," she whispered back, meeting his lips halfway. "I love you, Connal," she whimpered as he moved under her.

"I love you," he said huskily. "Oh, God, I love you more than my own life...!" He heard her shocked gasp and said it again and again, his hands insistent, demanding as he rocked her, lifted and pushed her in a rhythm that eventually shook the floor and the heavens.

She trembled uncontrollably. So did he. The explosion they'd kindled had all but landed them on the floor. He laughed huskily, lifting his head to meet her wickedly amused eyes.

"So much for new techniques borne of desperation," he murmured. "Now let's go upstairs and do it properly."

Hours later she nestled her cheek against his damp chest and opened her eyes. "We really ought to get dressed. Dad will be home eventually."

He kissed her forehead lazily. "I locked the door, remember?"

"So you did." She sighed, loving the new closeness they were sharing. "Harden said you were jealous of Evan."

"I was. Blind jealous, of him, of Hale, of any man who came near you. All these years together, and I didn't know that I loved you. Evan knew it instantly. And when I realized it, it was almost too late to stop you from getting an annulment." He shook her gently. "God, you've led me a merry chase! Even our first time, I was convinced that you were just curious about sex. I didn't think you gave a damn about me except physically."

"I've loved you since the first time I saw you," she whispered. "You became my world."

His arm tightened around her. "You were mine, too. It just took a while for me to realize it. Until that happened, I said some pretty harsh things to you. I hope in time you'll be able to forget them. I was running as fast as I could. It's taken me a long time to get over Marsha, but I think I have. I had to be whole again before I had anything to offer you. I had to stop being afraid of commitment, and it wasn't easy."

"Dad said that. I wasn't so optimistic. I thought you hated me."

"Wanted you, not hated you. And resented it like hell. Eventually you stayed on my mind so much that I burned from morning till night wanting you. It's becoming an obsession."

"Wanting isn't loving."

He chuckled. "I know that, too, but you have to admit, it's a big part of it." He kissed her closed eyelids. "I'd die for you, Penelope," he whispered huskily. "Will that do?"

"Oh, yes." She nuzzled her head against his chin. "Why did you call Edie?"

"I thought we'd come to that," he said, and grinned. "Evan told me what she was up to, so I phoned and told her that my marriage was perfectly legitimate and furthermore, I was desperately in love with my wife. I don't think we'll hear any more from her."

She lifted up, searching his face while he made a meal of her breasts with his eyes. "That's why Evan took me riding, to warn me that she'd called, looking for you!"

"Well, I'll be!" he burst out, diverted. "And he never said a word."

"Harden said you were jealous," she murmured dryly. "That gave me the first hope I'd had."

"How do you think I felt that night we spent together when you grumbled about Edie?" he laughed softly. "God, I'll never forget the way we made love then!" he whispered at her temple.

"Neither will I." She looked down into his eyes, her own fever kindling as she stared at him, her body tautening visibly. "Connal..." she whispered, her voice shaking.

His jaw tautened. He caught her waist and lifted her over him, pulling her down on his hips. "Yes," he whispered. "I need you, too. Again, little one."

"I don't think I can, this way..." she hesitated.

"Yes, you can," he said huskily. "I'll teach you. Like this, Pepi..."

She was shocked to discover that she could, indeed, and it was a long time before she was able to get up and dress afterward.

"Shy little country girl, hmmm?" he mused as they sat in the dining room sipping coffee and eating apple pie. "What an about-face!"

"It's the company I'm keeping," she murmured. "And we have a problem."

"You're pregnant?" he asked hopefully.

"That isn't a problem, and I may be but I don't know yet," she said. "I mean, we're married, but I don't have a wedding ring."

He grinned and pulled a box out of his jeans pocket. "Don't you?"

He held it out and she opened it, producing a beautiful set of rings—one with a big diamond, the other a gold band with inlaid diamonds that matched it.

"It's lovely," she said huskily. "But where's yours?" She glared at him. "You're wearing a ring, Connal Cade

Tremayne. I won't have every lonely spinster in south Texas trying to trespass on my preserves!"

"Well, well," he murmured dryly. "Okay. We'll go into town and buy me one."

The front door slammed and her father came walking into the dining room, stopping suddenly. "My God!" he wailed.

"You noticed my rings, did you?" Pepi grinned.

"Tell him that we're moving into the vacant house this afternoon, that'll unfreeze him," Connal dared.

"We are," she told her father. She frowned. "What's the matter with you? Aren't you happy that our marriage is going to work out and Connal and I are going to live together and you're going to have grandchildren at last? Aren't you happy about all that?"

"Of course I am, Pepi," he groaned. "It's just..."

"Just?" Connal prompted.

"Just?" Pepi seconded.

"Damn it," he raged, slamming his hat down. "You've eaten my apple pie!"

Several weeks later, Pepi made him a present of three freshly baked pies and the news that he was going to become a grandfather. She told Connal afterward that she wasn't sure which of her presents made him smile the widest.

* * * * *

⟨image⟩ *Diamond Jubilee Collection*

It's our 10th Anniversary...
and *you* get a present!

This collection of early Silhouette
Romances features novels written
by three of your favorite authors:

ANN MAJOR—*Wild Lady*
ANNETTE BROADRICK—*Circumstantial Evidence*
DIXIE BROWNING—*Island on the Hill*

* These Silhouette Romance titles were first published in the early 1980s
  and have not been available since!

* Beautiful Collector's Edition bound in antique green simulated leather to
  last a lifetime!

* Embossed in gold on the cover and spine!

✂ **PROOF OF PURCHASE**

Double your reading pleasure this fall with two Award of Excellence titles written by two of your favorite authors.

Available in September

DUNCAN'S BRIDE
by Linda Howard
Silhouette Intimate Moments #349

Mail-order bride Madelyn Patterson was nothing like what Reese Duncan expected—and everything he needed.

Available in October

THE COWBOY'S LADY
by Debbie Macomber
Silhouette Special Edition #626

The Montana cowboy wanted a little lady at his beck and call—the "lady" in question saw things differently....

These titles have been selected to receive a special laurel—the Award of Excellence. Look for the distinctive emblem on the cover. It lets you know there's something truly wonderful inside!

SILHOUETTE·INTIMATE·MOMENTS®

**Premiering in September,
a captivating new cover
for Silhouette's most adventurous
series!**

Every month, Silhouette Intimate Moments sweeps
you away with four dramatic love stories rich in
passion. Silhouette Intimate Moments presents
love at its most romantic, where life is exciting
and dreams do come true.

**Look for the new cover next month,
wherever you buy Silhouette® books.**

2IMNC-1

 Silhouette Books®